ALTHOUGH WE SHOULDN'T

ALTHOUGH WE SHOULDN'T

GWEN PARKS

Although We Shouldn't

Copyright 2024
By Gwen Parks Publishing

ALL RIGHTS RESERVED

No part of this book, whether in electronic form or physical book form, may be reproduced, copied, sold, or distributed in any way. That includes electronic, mechanical, photocopying, recording, or any other form of information sharing, storage, or retrieval system without the clear lawful permission of the author.

This book is a work of total and complete fiction. **No AI tools, programs, or apps were used in any part of creating this work.** This story was ideated and written directly from the author's imaginative and curious brain.

Edits: Amy Briggs, www.editsbyamy.com
Cover Design: Oh so Novel designs

1

WILLOW

A kiss is never just a kiss.

From the first contact of eager, trembling lips, and wistful sighs, a kiss has all the implications of could'ves, would'ves, and should'ves. It can say everything you want or need to say when words fail. Because, if I'm being honest, words seemed to have failed me all the time. When I was sixteen and green with envy that Stevie Jacobs was paying a little more attention to my rival Jessica Nixon, I wanted to tell Stevie that what he was looking for would never be found up Jessica's skirt. But instead, it was staring right in front of his eyes. Fear kept my down-turned, pouty lips sealed as I watched from my favorite spot underneath the willow tree one summer afternoon, while he whispered something in her ear that made her giggle. My heart had soured as it dropped to the depth of my unsettled stomach. My eyes brimmed with tears that I struggled to hold back, barely holding myself together. I envisioned us spending the summer together holding hands, going steady, and discovering what love was. I would have given him my favorite woven bracelet to wear, so he'd always have something to remember me by. I would see him all summer, and we would steal kisses underneath the same tree I had stood rooted in when I saw everything go down. The moment I saw him kiss her unabashedly as he held her face in his hands, I knew that those dreams I held close to my heart would never become true. That was the first lesson I had when I learned a kiss wasn't just a kiss. When Stevie kissed her, it was a direct message to my heart. It told me I was foolishly dreaming, and it was time to move on.

I tugged on my new blue denim shorts and played with the distressed ends until they snapped off as tears silently streamed down my face. I spent that summer single, heartbroken, but not alone. My best friend Serena had held my hand when I saw them walk by, and brought me to my favorite pizza place, where we ate our weight in Toni's famous deep-dish pizza with the ooey gooey cheese that melted with each bite you took, and marinara sauce that you could taste by smell alone. She was the person I gave my bracelet to, vowing always to have each other's back over guys.

Now that I had someone new in my life, things still haven't changed. She was my best friend and had been there for me through everything, so it was not a surprise she was on my mind right now, ten years later, as a kiss told me everything I had wanted to hear my entire life. It told me I was his and his heart belonged to only me. I opened my mouth greedily as I held onto him and took all that he gave me. This kiss made my toes curl and my heart hum in pleasure simultaneously. My body wilted as his hands explored my body like a man on a mission. He knew every hidden alley and terrain on my body. We spent an entire summer getting to know the maps of each other bodies and the little places that made us moan with just one touch. And when we conquered that, we spent an entire year exploring each other

Although We Shouldn't

souls. My best friend crept in my thoughts again as he pushed down the straps of my bra and unclasped the hooks to expose my breasts to him. My nipples pointed at him like missiles, preparing to launch at him.

I wanted to tell my best friend about the man I was undeniably in love with.

But as reality, the evil bitch that she was, would have it, I couldn't tell my best friend—at least not yet. As much as she loved me to pieces and wanted to see me happy, she wouldn't understand the choices I made. She wouldn't see what I see when I looked at his caramel eyes that darkened right before he kissed me or when he was saying something that would rock my world, from his dirty promises to his sweet whispers. It broke my heart that I wasn't able to share this with her. So, it became our secret.

His lips latched onto my sensitive nipples and eradicated all wayward thoughts I previously had. I moaned as his strong hands massaged the other breast to give it equal attention. My head lolled back. "James," I moaned. I used to worry about the rough callouses on his hands, afraid it would scrape against my skin and feel wrong as he touched my most intimate areas.

He told me, "Relax, baby. I'll make you feel good."

It was the first time I trusted him, and I never looked back.

His callouses smoothed over my nipples and I let out another moan. I fell back onto my bed as my body caved underneath the allure of his touch and pulled him down with me. My legs wrapped around his waist, trapping him between my legs. I was sure he could smell my arousal through my jeans. The blue thong I was wearing just for him was soaked just enough to leave me in a desperate state of want. The sexual anticipation had me rubbing against his thick thigh, which was perfectly placed to create the friction

I needed to alleviate the burn that was building up inside me. He could just look at me and I was ready for him—wet and needy, filled with anticipation. I wanted him to fuck me on every surface in my room like he had on my birthday last summer. He made me come so hard, I thought I'd die from sheer pleasure alone. I wanted to experience that again with him, in his arms, over and over again. But we didn't have time to explore each other how we wanted. In one hour, we had somewhere to be where our presence was mandatory. And we were very much a well-hidden secret, so we couldn't use each other as an excuse to be late.

He growled; his frantic hands pulling at the buttons of my jeans. I felt his touch everywhere. I must've been high on ecstasy, the erotic kind, because I felt his touch in places I never had before. In the back of my mind, I knew our feelings heightened our experiences together. Every time we reconnected, it drove me to new extremes. I heard the impatience in his labored breathing and the way his hair fell in his face made him seem like some kind of fallen God. Lord only knows how hard the fall from heaven must've been. I couldn't believe he was mine. His touch might have been all lust as his hands dragged my jeans down my legs and exposed the blue thong I wore just for him.

Blue as in his favorite color.

Blue as the ocean we made love in last summer as we escaped reality for a weekend.

But when his eyes connected with mine, no matter what he was doing, his eyes always gentled and showed the depths of his love for me. It never changed, and I craved it as much as I craved his touch, when he plunged his two digits inside my wet pussy. When I felt the head of his massive dick against my thigh. By the time our clothes were finally removed, and we were skin-to-skin, I exhaled heavily. I could never get enough of the feeling of him on top of me.

Although We Shouldn't

My breath became labored and choppy. His eyes stayed on me; mine remained on him.

It was always like this with us.

"Eternity," he whispered to me. I felt his dick nudge my entrance. Bare. We never wanted any barriers between us. To be honest, I felt closest to him without the protection.

Tears prickled at my eyes but never fell. "Eternity," I whispered back. Those words are what we promised each other because we knew our relationship came with its own sets of struggles. We were ready to face it together, though. We whispered this word to each other every time we had sex. It was the only moment he gave me that was soft. Because after that, he gave me all of him—rough, dirty, and unchained.

He plunged through me, filling me so full and intense that there wasn't any space in me he hadn't filled. My walls gripped him, almost a direct mimic of how my arms were around him, never wanting to let go. I held in my moan as I matched his thrusts with equal amounts of vigor and speed. My teeth latched onto his shoulder, and I bit down on him, which caused him to let out a hiss. A smile played on my lips, satisfied with his response. I loved knowing I could drive him as crazy as he did to me. One of his hands held onto mine and placed them atop my head, while the other went to my throat. The perfect combination of sweet and rough. "Are you gonna milk my dick, baby girl?" His voice sent shivers down my spine. My eyes closed involuntarily, letting the full power of his voice take over me, and I let out another moan. His hands squeezed my throat once, in a warning. He wanted an answer and wouldn't settle for less.

His demanding side coming out in full force.

"Yes," I rasp out. My free hand pulls on his hair. His intoxicating scent is all over my room. I revel in the woodsy scent mixed in with oil from his job as a mechanic. From the first kiss we shared, I always loved his scent. Maybe even a little before that. It's a whole other playing field to become obsessed with the one person you love. He drove into me again before placing another rough kiss on my puffy lips. I gave myself completely to him as he pumped into me, bending me to his will.

Thrust. Squeeze. Kiss. And repeat. The rhythm he set had me close to the edge before he pulled out of me entirely and grabbed my face to kiss me. "I'm not done with you yet." His smirk promised more, even though we both knew we were running out of time. It both thrilled and scared me how much we pushed our luck by stealing time. These brief moments where it was just him and I, and we weren't as careful with our words or actions with each other. Having a secret affair can be fun when it's just sex. But when you have your heart on the line, it's like living in an insulated bubble that slowly steals the air you need to live. Your lungs squeeze and your chest waves in from the pressure.

When you're in love, it's about living in the moment—all the moments, and declaring your love for one another whenever the moment seizes you. But we can't do that, so we steal time to do it in secret.

He spun me around and had me on my hands and knees. I felt the sweep of air as his hand moved to give my ass a rough smack. His hand landed on the sensitive skin of my ass again, which had my arousal leaking down my leg. Now my room was filled with the smell of sex and James. My second favorite smell next to the smell of Jason after he's come back from work. By the time we had sex the first time around, he had me addicted to sex with him. Before him, I wasn't a prude by any means. I had what I liked to call a healthy sexual appetite. But with someone as experienced as him, as usual, it took things to another level. "I fucking love the feeling of your pussy claiming my dick," his tongue licked the shell of my ear. His breath was against my neck as he

Although We Shouldn't

wrapped my dark tresses around his hand and gave a gentle pull to have my head looking up at him. His look was feral, like a Viking ready to destroy a town. But the only thing he was set to destroy was my pussy. I couldn't wait. I was his for the taking. "God, your pussy was made for me. It wraps around me like a glove."

My ass bounced back, eagerly waiting for him to plunder into me again. Only, it wasn't his penis that entered me, but his two digits. My greedy pussy sucked his fingers in as he fucked me with them. He entered another finger in as his thumb rubbed my clit in tandem. It was a delicious experience he created just for me. I could feel and hear my juices gathering, he continued his ministrations. My impending orgasm was coming, I could feel it as my legs buckled under the pressure.

"There it is," he rasped as he sped up his fingers. I looked back at him as my eyes glazed over. His eyes held a mischievous glint and a wide smirk. "Come for me, right now." he gave me another bruising kiss and did a swivel motion that had me breaking apart.

I moaned long and loud, my mouth open and my eyes shut as wave after wave of pleasure rocketed through me. If this was the only time I could be free to express how much I love this man until the next time we could sneak away, I was going to do so limitlessly. I didn't have time to think before, I felt him at my entrance, and he drove back into me. His arms banded around me and were flush against my breasts. I felt each thrust as if it were the chords of a guitar playing the sweetest music I've ever heard, where the sounds of our lovemaking were the music and the sounds of us coming together were the encore.

We had a few seconds to bask in the afterglow before we untangled from each other. Our panting breaths commingled with one another. His arms reached out to tuck me into him and rested his chin on top of my head. I wanted to stay like this forever, where nothing could stop us from doing what we did best—loving each other, where nothing could harm us. A somber smile graced his beautiful face because we both knew once we walked out the front door, it wouldn't be together, and we were back to acting like we didn't just celebrate our engagement in the last ten minutes. I'd have to endure one hundred and twenty pain-staking minutes where people would try to set him back up with his ex, while I stood several paces away from him. And while his ex was a lovely woman, I loved her to pieces. she wasn't me. They shouldn't be trying to set him up like he was single. They should congratulate him because he was officially off the market. My heart stuttered in my chest, leaving a melancholy feeling to wash over me.

As if he could hear the warring thoughts in my head, like he too knew what we would walk into, he whispered, "It'll be okay, Willaford." James always called me by my full name when he had to soothe away my frayed edges. He called me my first name after he first kissed me and thought I was horrified by it. He used it again when he told me he loved me over the phone, in a whispered voice, because he was around people who didn't know our truth. And once more, when we first had to act like nothing had happened the day after we had sex. I was devastated when I watched him move around me when the night before he had my body doing all types of tricks in different angles and wrung me dry. He had said something so mundane that no one would question it, but it was the use of my full name that caught my attention, that let me know he was in it—this—with me. I wasn't alone. He said, "Pass the jam, Willaford." I looked up and met his eyes, startled that he was speaking to me in front of everyone, and saw the hunger in his eyes, but also, compassion. He knew what I

Although We Shouldn't

was going through, what I was feeling. Because he felt the same way.

His thumb brushed away an errant tear, bringing me back to the present, as his eyes mirrored my pain. "We'll tell them soon, and we won't have to hide behind closed doors anymore. Then everyone will know you're mine."

"But when?" Because when was the perfect time to turn somebody's world upside down? Why was it that turning our world right side up meant everyone else was left as a casualty? I wondered how Serena would feel when she found out. I imagined it would be awkward at first, and we'd stumble around words to explain to each other how we felt about it all. But I had to have hope she'd eventually be happy for me, for us. Right?

I needed her to accept this because the alternative wasn't something I wanted to wrap my head around.

He sighed. As unfair as it was to demand an answer like that from him without taking into consideration what could happen to his life, since it would affect him more than it would me, it was also unfair to me to always wonder what if and hold my breath. We needed a plan to tell everyone about our relationship. Yes, it was unconventional. But it was also raw, passionate, and real. And it was ours.

"After this week, when everyone has time to settle down from celebrating, we can get everyone together and tell them." The light gray in his eyes stood out as he pressed his forehead to mine. I wanted to stay this way forever. With the sun's rays casting a soft glow over us in my bedroom. His scent encased my senses and him right by my side. It was a novel idea, a grand idea even, to skip tonight and keep us locked away forever. We wouldn't have to leave the confines of this room, and we'd survive on our love alone.

I knew he wouldn't want to do that, though.

He's a man who faces things head-on. And I knew no

matter what I suggested and how tempting it might sound, we were doomed to face reality. Gathering him in my arms once more, I held onto him before he had to leave. I had a sinking feeling in my gut that this would be the last time we would have with each other. A moment so peaceful and still and perfect. I held onto this feeling, so I could look back on it on the days when it would be hard to put one foot in front of the other.

Because once everyone knew, all hell would break loose. Especially with Serena.

How else was she supposed to react when she found out I was marrying her father?

2

JAMES

Awareness ripples through my body as the sun beams down through the slits of my sage green curtains from my bedroom window and warms me from the inside out. My limbs stretch as I slowly come out of my slumber, my joints cracking as I get my bearings. Long, lean legs wrap around my waist, and a dainty arm lands on my chest, as the owner of the most beautiful heart inches closer to me in her sleep. I smile inwardly at the sight before me. My body heats at the contact, and I tug her closer. I cherish these small pockets of time I have with her uninterrupted where I don't have to worry about anything outside my door. My heart does its usual kick-start pattern of pound, pound, flutter whenever *she's* around me.

Willow.

I don't always get to start my days like this, lying in leisure and not hurrying around like a chicken with its head cut off. I get to take my time with her. Relax. Indulge in the pleasures of quality time. We often have to plan and maneuver time together away from people to avoid them asking questions about us and why we're spending so much time together alone. We skillfully hid our love from my ex-wife, my kids, and anyone who knows us who might let it leak to them about us.

The age gap between us makes it hard for people to accept us, and the unconventional way we got together will be hard for people to swallow, especially for Elaine, my ex-wife. I hated having to look over our shoulders like common thieves and criminals when the only thing I ever stole was Willow's heart.

Nothing about us should make sense. Her pieces shouldn't fit my jagged hard edges. But they do in the most unique and beautiful way. She doesn't make me feel young, she makes me feel alive. With the way she spritzes through life with no plans and asks questions later. The way she freely gives herself to those she cares about and expects nothing in return. Her surprising sense of humor can draw the deepest full belly laugh from me. She centers me in a way that can instantly calm me down. The way she listens first and then offers her advice. I saw what Serena saw in her as a friend, but ten times more. The way she had me so entirely wrapped around her finger and she didn't even have to lift it.

If I could have predicted this was the way my life would end up, I could never in my wildest dreams have guessed it would have ended up this way. But with every dip, twist, and turn, I would do it all over again for the same outcome.

With her.

Willow's unique scent of peaches and spice wraps around me as I breathe it in like it's the last time I'll ever get the chance to. It always feels like I'm on borrowed time, so I soak in as much of her as I can while I have the opportunity. My hand brushes through Willow's long blonde mane as I peer down at her while she rests peacefully on me. Her lashes

Although We Shouldn't

flutter as her eyeballs flit around her closed lids. We had to sneak away last night after hanging out with my family to finesse our way to my apartment last night.

She had left first, claiming she had an early morning and couldn't stay any longer, and I left two hours behind so I wouldn't raise any suspicion. No one questioned the timing of it as I slipped out and said my goodbyes. We celebrated my daughter's birthday. My only daughter. Willow's best friend. I'm hoping after next week, not only will we not have to hide away from anyone and sneak furtive glances at each other from across the room, but we will love each other out in the open. Without any alibis needed. It might be too much to ask, but I'm also hoping everyone will be happy for us despite any reservations they may have.

That they'll see we belong together.

Next to Willow, my family—my kids—are the most important thing to me. The thought of hurting them with the news of my relationship with Willow has kept me up for so many nights with my hand wrapped around an old family portrait, wondering if we'd make it through the scandal.

I hate to think of Willow and me as anything but a loving relationship, but realistically, this will shock everyone.

The last picture we took before we told the kids about our divorce is the picture I hold close to my heart. It's a constant reminder of what matters most. I keep it in my wallet whenever things get tough for me. The picture shows a simpler time when things made sense and there wasn't any pain in anyone's eyes. It took some time for us to create a new normal with my family after I divorced their mom.

Although they were well over eighteen when it happened, they still were upset. My kids had this distorted idea of us in their heads—that everything was perfect, and Elaine and I would be together forever and were madly in love. It was true for a while, until it wasn't. The truth is, we had been having issues for about a year before we made the untimely decision. Things weren't bad. They were terrible. We argued constantly over anything. We stressed each other out. And Elaine had an affair.

Our kids didn't understand the split, largely because Elena and I made a point to keep our marital troubles on the down low. We didn't want to disrupt their lives and drag them in the middle of our issues. We certainly didn't want them to feel like they had to pick a side. If there's anything I'm grateful for is that Elena and I always put our kids' best interests first. And now that they're adjusted to this normal, I can't help but feel protective of that newfound peace we've created through strained smiles and watery laughs.

But I can't have it at the expense of my new relationship.

At the expense of breaking Willow's heart.

She is the one person I refuse to give up. Her smile is the reason I get up every morning and her scent is what I smell every day that makes my heartbeat incessantly. Every day I'm away from her feels like my heart has been pulled out of my chest. My heart cavity is ruined by the strain caused by the physical distance we have to keep from each other.

I finally found love again.

After feeling like I wouldn't for so long after the divorce.

I had given up all hope that I'd be happy again and thought I was perfectly happy with just being okay. I had my stable job as the sole owner of James's Auto Shop. After working in the corporate world, where I traveled nonstop and made rich people even more rich, I was tired of that life, and had invested in enough stock to comfortably retire while still making passive income. But I still wanted to work. I wanted to get my hands dirty and help real people. The people in my community. So, I started my car repair business and made my dad's dream come true. I had my

Although We Shouldn't

two beautiful kids. Greyson was working in a top IT firm and Serena graduated college debt-free, thanks in part to my old job as a partner in a law firm. Dating apps were never my thing, especially at the age of 42. I haven't been on a date since the first four years of my marriage with Elaine.

The dating scene had drastically changed since I last seriously dated anyone. I'm a one-woman kind of guy. I had no business dating multiple people at one time. I barely had time to get a full night's rest. I had gone on a couple of blind dates set up from the guys at the shop and they all had a good laugh at my three awful date stories.

After that, I tapped out and said enough was enough.

I had settled into the fact I had caught a lucky break with my ex and people only had one true love. I lost mine. I accepted that. Never in a million years did I think I'd find a shooting star twice. And not in the way it happened either. Slow at first like a trickling stream of water then all at once like a freight train, and all I could do was hold on.

As it came closer to the time to come clean to my family about the sudden change in my life, troubling thoughts plagued my mind, keeping me up late at night. What if they couldn't accept it, us? What if it tore my family apart, and I was forced to choose between my family and Willow? I didn't know if I could choose. Both were extremely, and equally, important in my life. If it came down to it, I wasn't sure what I would do.

Movement shifts the sheets as my eyes land on Willow's sleeping form. My healed heart clamored in my chest begging me to stay in bed and wake up her up with my tongue on her tight, pink, pussy. Holding my hardening dick, I groan. Now was not the time to be acting like a horny teenager. I had other things I planned on doing today. Carefully, as to not wake her, I slid from underneath the blanket, quietly slipped out of the room, and closed the bedroom door behind me.

If I knew her well enough, which I did, she'd wake up and claim she was dying of hunger and pilfer through my cabinets, wearing nothing but one of my old t-shirts and look for something to eat. She'd stretch on her tiptoes with her ass cheeks playing peekaboo with me, her perky little ass swaying ever so slightly, and begging me to grab a huge chunkful and squeeze. She'd tease me about my survivalist skills, since I always opt for take-out food. With an impish smile on her face, she would say, "You don't ever have anything to eat." Because it was always implied that I could always eat her out for breakfast. And as much as I like to take her up on that offer today, I had something else in mind.

She's been very anxious about when we'd fess up and let everyone know—little gentle prods to get a date out of me. I think all the secrecy has been catching up to her and honestly, it's been wearing on me too. I yearn for the day when I can lay a kiss on her and not risk a heart attack because someone found out before we were ready.

No.

We wouldn't wait any longer than we'd have to. Over a fresh bouquet of roses and a nice romantic breakfast, we can discuss how we'll tell everyone.

Next weekend.

Because if either of us wait any longer, someone will find out the wrong way and blow everything we worked for to crap.

Willow deserves better than that.

Although We Shouldn't

I always hated going to the grocery store.

As a man, I am simple by nature. If it's good, then I buy it. There were way too many options to choose from that made things so much harder to pick the right choice. It was a perfect symbol of the way people dated now. When I was married, Elaine did all the shopping. I didn't have to worry about gluten-free this or dairy-free that. And what was the difference between pasture-raised eggs or not?

So many signs glared at me in red and claimed it was the best sale ever.

Yeah, right. And I'm the Queen of England.

None of that mattered to me though. All I cared about was picking the right breakfast produce to make Willow that would put a smile on her face. This is one of the first times I'm attempting to actually cook, and I would cut my right hand off before I accidentally poisoned her from my cooking.

As I walked down the produce aisle, I placed a carton of eggs in my shopping cart before moving down to the fruit—strawberries. I needed strawberries. That was the safest bet. With a little whipped cream and feeding each other, I could see a thousand different ways to romance her and have her in my bed. My dick grows uncomfortably in my pants at the image of eating whipped cream off her smooth body. Looking both ways to make sure no one was around, I discreetly adjusted my pants.

Yep.

Definitely strawberries.

I add one more pack just to be cautious.

We both had a healthy appetite.

After placing them in my cart, I head down two aisles. Reading the labels for the sections, I searched for pancake mix. I couldn't make it from scratch, but I could definitely follow directions. My feet glided swiftly through the supermarket and my eyes fixed on the signs above. Checking the time on my watch, I deduced I had another twenty minutes before Willow woke up, so I needed to hurry.

But of course, the universe hated me.

"James?" the soft cadence of Elaine's voice stopped me in my tracks.

I could pretend I didn't hear her, but we finally can talk to each other without biting each other's head off. I wouldn't want to risk upsetting her and putting myself back two paces. So, reluctantly, I turned around and greeted the mother of my kids.

"Hey, what are you doing here?" Stupid. What else would she be doing here?

"Just shopping for the church's bake sale." She laughs lightly, pushing her cart closer to me. "You know they love my baking." She swipes a lock of her jet-black hair behind her ear.

"You were always good in the kitchen. Dinner. Dessert. It was all good." There—a compliment. I can't go wrong there.

"Yeah," she sighs wistfully. "I don't have anyone else to cook for now that the kids have moved out. So, I volunteer for a lot of events to show off my skills." She hesitates for a second. Something is on her mind. I just don't know what.

After a minute of silence, I tip my head to her and turn back to my cart, but her hand on my arm stops me again. I used to feel shivers at her touch. Now it's nothing but familiarity. It's in a way that says, we used to love each other, but now we both just love our kids.

"Serena was telling me a few days ago how she misses our family vacations. I was thinking, now that we're civil again, we can plan something this summer." There's a lilt at the end of her sentence like she's not quite sure she should say it but can't help herself. It feels weird, I realize. This small little truce we have when we were once at each other's throats. Its taken a while to get here, but I don't exactly hate it. She's testing the waters. Seeing how much we can withstand.

Thinking on my feet, I nod my head. "How about next weekend, we head to the family cabin and have everyone down there. It'll be the perfect weather for it." And the perfect place to break the news. My mind is already running with a thousand different ways to tell them—in the morning over breakfast, in the afternoon, as the sun beams down on us and we're out hiking in nature, or maybe at night over a roaring fire while everyone settled for the night. The options are endless.

Elaine's eyes brighten, "Oh that soon." She fidgets with the bracelets on her arms. "I was thinking you could think it over before you had an answer."

Fuck. Am I pushing it? "Unless you think it's too soon and we can plan for later in the summer." It wouldn't be ideal to wait another couple of months. But we can make do. I hope.

She flushes. "No, it's perfect. Perfect."

"You sure?" She seems nervous. Her eyes roam around the store as we stand here longer.

"Positive," Her hand reaches out before lowering it back down awkwardly. She laughs nervously.

I clear my throat. 'Good, then it's settled."

"You wouldn't mind if I came along?" She peeks at me through her lashes. We haven't all been in the same room for a while. With our new co-parenting system, they've both shuffled between us. Sharing time and holidays with the kids. Plus, they're old enough now to not need supervision. Mostly.

"The kids will be thrilled you're there. I'm sure we could last one weekend away from the world and just reconnect and update everyone on what's going on in our lives."

"Good." She smiles. "Well, I won't take up too much of your time. It was nice seeing you."

"Same." I turn back to my cart and speed through the rest of my shopping list before paying for my things and heading back home. I can't wait to tell Willow the plan. The opportunity just fell in our laps. Everything will go perfectly.

After all, what could go wrong?

3

JAMES
TWO YEARS AND 5 MONTHS AGO

The sound of the floorboards on the stairs creaks ever so quietly in the dead of night. Aside from the hum of the refrigerator, the house has been eerily quiet, a blessed reprieve from the chaos with Elaine earlier today. I feel the *thump thump thump* of my building headache pulsing on the side of my head. My body tenses, bracing myself for whoever is coming down the stairs. I secretly hope it's not my wife. And that's an awful thing to say. To think.

I know.

But something is off—between us, her and I. It has been for a while now. Our vibe, our rhythm isn't what it used to be. I used to be able to predict what would make her happy. Over time, those things turned more into a monetary value and if I didn't deliver, then all hell would break loose. Not tears. If it was tears, I could handle it. I would turn on our wedding song "The Way You Look Tonight" and slow dance with her as we build a new version of what she'd want. I was good at turning her tears into water laughs. Those were manageable. Instead, I received her ire.

She snipes at me constantly all day. Whether it's about the

chores in the house or some new vacation she wants, it has always put me on high alert. My skin would feel too tight, and the air would leave my lungs choking me. She hadn't always been that way and a part of me blames myself for the disillusion of our marriage. After all, it takes two, right? My heart pulses in my chest, causing a dull ache that doesn't seem to quit anytime I think something I shouldn't like maybe we just won't work. Maybe this is the end of our marriage. Maybe I'm not fit for a marriage. That leaves me here, in my current predicament.

Hiding from her. Even if it's just for a few short moments at night when everyone is sleeping helps me keep the stress away. After all, my doctor said my stress test wasn't looking so good. After I nearly had a stroke last week, I went to see my doctor to see what the cause could be. It all came down to stress. Either I quit my job, which if my recent credit card bills from Elaine's recent shopping trip were any indication to go by, I couldn't do anytime soon, or we split up. And I didn't want to do that. She was the love of my life. I spent my twenties loving her. So, I can suck it up, be a man and spend my forties caring for her. In the only way I know how, financially. Because lord knows I can't do anything else right.

The small sounds of soft footsteps echo in the silence, but it might as well be a gunshot with the way my heart is pounding. I depend on these moments alone so I can decompress from the day away from prying eyes. My eyes squeeze shut as I focus on my breathing and lean my forearms on the counter, thinking of ways I can discreetly hide the cup of bourbon I poured myself twenty minutes ago.

I don't need another person prying into the why's of my actions.

"Oh, I didn't know anyone else was up." A soft voice filters into the kitchen. My shoulder deflates—not my wife.

It makes me a prick for even feeling the slightest bit relieved but that's where we're at now.

I turn around and face the person who invited them into my kitchen and fold my arms against my chest. I'm met with puffy blue eyes and a red nose. Willow. Serena's best friend. Conceding my time alone is over, I walk over to the cupboard that holds the mugs and start the makings of a hot chocolate. Despite it being the summer, I know this is the only thing that would make the girls feel better after crying their eyes out. No matter what the weather looked like. Once the hot cocoa is made, I pass it to her, and her fingers reach out to take it from me. Her hand grazes mine in passing and soft tingles shoot up my arms.

Fucking weird.

Must be the static, my mind reasons.

She accepts the cup graciously as she blows a tentative breath to cool off the liquid. "Thanks." She eyes me curiously over her mug as she leans on the opposite side of the kitchen. "What are you doing up this late?"

"I can ask you the same thing." I offer in return.

"Touche," she laughs lightly, though it's a bit watery. My hand itches to hold my own cup, but I refuse to drink in front of her. "I just got broken up with," she says after a while.

I feel bad for her. I wish I could tell her that it'll get easier. But what do I know? I can't even fix my marriage to save my life, and that's supposed to be forever. The best I can offer her is, "It doesn't get easier over time."

She chuckles, taking a lengthy sip of her hot cocoa. "Do men ever grow up?" She sighs wearily.

"Afraid not. It's all games and beer, with a slight variation in sports interests. Even I am not able to escape the insanity of men's foolish behavior from time to time." I internally wince thinking of how I had practically yelled in the house at

Elaine for expecting too much out of me. I don't think anyone was around to hear since we were throwing a pool party outside. But our walls aren't one hundred percent soundproof, so it could have traveled. Do I regret my words? Yes. But I was at my wits end, and it didn't seem like she was getting me at all.

"Please don't say that. I need a little hope." She groans playfully. She flops over the nearest counter dramatically and holds her hand over her face but is careful to not spill her drink.

"Sorry to break it to you. But we men are not that evolved. Sometimes we slip and say things don't mean." I curse silently. Because that would be the stupid thing to do. Vent about my marital troubles to my daughter's best friend. I hope she doesn't notice my slip-up and brushes it away.

She smiled apologetically. "If it makes you feel better, she seems to have gotten over it fairly quickly." Nothing but kindness and empathy bleeds from her words and I don't expect anything else from her. Willow has always been a kind soul, always offering help to those around her and lending a listening ear.

I still can't help but feel like a tool for being one of them, though.

There must be some imaginary rule that says I shouldn't be having these types of conversations with her right?

But instead of diverting the conversation, I dive a little deeper into the waters. "You saw that did you," I cringe. God, I hope she hadn't. Those were not my finest moments and we always make sure the kids aren't around to witness it. Willow may not be my kid, but she's kid adjacent.

"Just a little bit of it." Her forefinger and thumb pinch together to show how little she's heard. "Only because I have the bladder of a peanut and getting in a drinking competition with Greyson was the worst thing I could've done." She

Although We Shouldn't

chuckles awkwardly and lowers her face to the ground in shame.

"It's okay, I'm not mad," I don't think I am at least. Embarrassed? Sure. But mad? Questionable. I rub the back of my head and squeeze the nape to relieve the mounting pressure. "They don't have a clue how bad it's gotten do they?"

She looks up, slightly relieved, slightly shy. "No. I don't think so. They haven't mentioned anything. Not to me at least."

I sigh, relieved that at least we did one thing right. We should still be mindful of when and where we argue. That could have easily been Serena popping in for a makeup refresh or Greyson coming in to play video games. We don't want the kids to worry and ask about things that will never happen—like a divorce. *But is that true? Will we never get divorced? Isn't that what you've been thinking about?* My conscious whispers ideas I have no business considering. I knew what I signed up for when I promised Elaine forever. I don't have any right to opt-out now. I took my vows seriously. This is just a rough patch.

"I'd appreciate it if you could not say anything about today." Unless it's absolutely necessary, my kids don't need to know anything at all. Elaine and I may patch things up and the kids would have gotten worked up over nothing.

Willow nods her head in agreement and for the second time tonight, I'm relieved.

"So, is that why you're down here?" she asks tepidly. She's not prying, but just curious, I guess. The blues in her eyes soften from sympathy and I hate that it is there. I don't need anyone's sympathy. I need answers. And I guess that's what led me to answer her honestly again.

"Yeah. I needed time to myself to relieve stress," My hand goes to the cup of bourbon behind me, and I smile chargingly. "This is how I do it."

"A cup of alcohol and silence. Now that I can get behind." She smiles mischievously like she's in on a secret.

Something about the look in her eye that night made my blood pressure elevate more. Not that we were doing anything wrong, but that we were going to, or might. The implications choked me.

We spent that night talking about our woes and shared advice over hot cocoa and bourbon. I gave her advice on how to navigate men and she gave me advice on how to get on my wife's good side. It was all innocent and in good nature. And it started the first of many late-night chats with her.

Talking to Willow helped me through the summer. And in her, I found an unexpected friend. I learned although she was young—only twenty-two years old—she was wise beyond her years.

I don't know exactly what woke her up that night or if she never went to sleep at all. All I know is that whenever she slept over and we were both up with a restless mind she would wait for me with a cup of bourbon ready to drink while she sipped her hot cocoa.

———

"Dad, oh my god thank you!" Serena jumped up and down as she walked around her new car. She's been begging for one forever. She hated taking the metro or, God forbid, asking for a ride. She's made several arguments about how she's an adult and shouldn't have to rely on anyone else for transportation.

Elaine wanted her to earn a car, but I thought it was complete bullshit. Another thing she found to argue with me over. I decided to bite the bullet and get her a car. It's not completely new, but it is an updated model. It's a 2019 silver Jeep. A few years older than the original car she's been

Although We Shouldn't

hinting at. She works a nice job at the veterinary clinic and has been saving up with Willow to move out.

I thought she deserved a treat.

After all, we bought Greyson a car when he was her age.

"You like it?" I ask her, even though it's a moot point. It's very evident in the way she hasn't taken her eyes off the car and unlocked it to get in immediately that she loves the car. My chest swells with pride knowing I put a smile on my baby girl's face.

"This is perfect, dad! I can't wait to show Willow." She takes out her phone and screeches in the receiver and gushes. "Willow, you will not believe this." Her voice fades out as she drives away. I should've warned her about being on the phone and driving. But Willow doesn't live far so she should be safe.

A throat clears and the smell of vanilla and cocoa beans drifts in the air. The hair on the back of my neck rises and I look over my shoulder to see Elaine glaring at me with her hip cocked out.

"A car, really? What's that going to teach her?" derision coats her voice and feels like nails on a chalkboard.

I walk slowly over to her and ignore her words. Pasting on a saccharine sweet smile, I place a placid kiss on her forehead before saying, "That we want her to be happy and independent."

"She has a job, James. She can save up for a car instead of an apartment. We gave that choice to Greyson." Her stiletto heels echo in the hallways as she walks by me.

"Not everything should be a lesson. You used to know that." I beg her to understand. I hope she doesn't turn this into a fight. I refuse to feel bad for spoiling my daughter. My wife loves her kids. But lately, it's been "They have to learn the value of a dollar."

My kids are just fine,

They understand money doesn't grow on trees. And yes, I do spoil them. But I spoil my wife more, so it's funny that she says this now.

"For once, I'm not going to argue with you." I close the door softly behind me and lock it. It feels like a prison with just me and her in the house. My feet take me to the stairs as Elaine's eyes follow me as I walk up the stairs.

"Where are you going?" She huffs.

"To our bedroom. I'm tired after working overtime today. You're welcome to join me." I offer as an olive branch. Maybe we'll reconnect and laugh at how this whole argument is silly. Maybe she offers to join me in the shower instead. She's always loved to surprise me with a quickie, and now I'm using it as a bargaining chip.

She doesn't take the offer though.

Instead, she walks away.

4

WILLOW

"I can't believe my dad is seriously going to take us camping. We haven't done a family outing in forever." Serena's eyes light up. I've been on pins and needles all day ever since she called me to pack with her.

"So, you don't mind that I'm coming along with you guys?" My legs bounce up and down as I lean back on my arms on her bed. I've had this restless energy ever since we planned to tell everyone this weekend about our engagement. He assures me that everything will be fine and I'm overreacting. My gut has been eating at itself all day and building up the pressure the closer we get to the date.

Serena rolls her eyes as she hunts in her closet. "Are you kidding me? You're practically family anyway. It'll be great. We can share a room in the cabin and then we can stay up all night and you can tell me about the guy you're dating."

My heart stalls in my chest. I've been careful not to show any signs that I've been seeing anyone because then she'll ask questions. Questions I can't really answer right now. "What guy?" I hope that came off as calm and not anxious like how I feel inside.

"Oh, come on, Willow. You're always on your phone, whispering at night when you think I'm asleep and you always smile at your phone when you receive a text. It's honestly so awesome you found someone who can make you feel as good as David makes me feel." David is her fiancée. They just recently got engaged and I couldn't be happier for my bestie.

I use this as an opportunity to feel her out. I wouldn't say who the guy is, because let's face it, I'm a terrible liar. "Okay, so there is someone."

She shrieks in joy, "I knew it. I fucking knew it." She trots over to me and jumps on her bed. "Who is it? Do I know him? Oh, this will be so great. We can double date,"

I laugh easily, caught up in her excitement. Some of the nerves in my stomach ease. "What if he was older? Would you still be happy for me?"

"Honey, I don't care if he has a third nipple, I'd still be happy for you. Although you might have some fun with that." Her eyebrows wiggle up and down and I laugh harder and push her away. "Honestly, I was a little bit worried you were hung up on Steven. The guy was a total fuck boy. I was going to stage an intervention."

"Nope, definitely over him." And thank goodness for that. But if she knew how I got over him or who helped me get over him, I hope she'd still be happy.

"When do I get to meet him?" She turns to me expectantly. "I'm kind of miffed you waited this long to tell me."

"It's sort of complicated at the moment. But hopefully soon."

"Good, because you are not a secret, my dear girl. You are meant to be shown off to the world." She stands back up and walks back over to her closet to pick out clothes for the weekend trip.

"He's honestly the best guy I know. He makes my insides

Although We Shouldn't

all melty. I can't explain the feeling. It feels like coming home to a fireplace after playing in the snow all day." A soft smile graces my face thinking about him.

"God, you make me so jealous. But I totally understand how you feel. My David makes me feel the same way. But new love is honestly the best feeling in the world."

"It is," I agree softly.

"Okay, so spill all the details. I want to know everything. How'd you guys meet? God, what's his name?" She laughs as she steps out and holds a polka-dot blue sundress up to her chest.

"Definitely not camping material. We're going to be in the woods. Not at the mall." Serena is the fashionista out of us. If she could, she'd wear designer heels to the dentist. In fact, I think at one point she had.

"This is why you're my best friend. You make sure I don't look like a fool." She throws the dress to the ground and goes back into her closet. It's not as big as the one in her childhood home, but it's big enough to walk in. Honestly, with the extra closet spaces in the hall, they also opt as a closet for her. She has so many clothes and shoes she couldn't fit them all in her room.

Walking over to her I pick up a pair of cargo shorts of mine she borrowed for a boating trip. "These will be good. Something casual."

She turns around, inspecting what's in my hand and purses her lips. "I think I can work with this. It'll be jungle chic. But back to your boo thang. I need details. I'm dying over here."

Laughing softly, I give her one truth. "He's the love of my life. And aside from you, he's my best friend."

"I would be jealous, again," She laughs with me. "But David is my best friend too. Does he treat you well?" She digs out a pale blue camisole that would look great on her with the shorts and looks for my approval.

I give her a thumbs up. "He treats me like a princess. We honestly came back from a trip to the Hamptons, and we lounged all day at the beach and drank endless amounts of wine and laughed at everything and nothing at all."

"You hussy. So that's where you went." Her hand goes to her chest in mock appall. "Everything is finally going great. My parents are getting along again. I think I've even seen my dad smile a time or two. I'm happily engaged, and my best friend is in love. As long as Greyson has a soccer ball in his hands, he's fine with everything."

My heart skips a beat at the mention of her dad. Soon, we won't have to hide our love from the people closest to us and we can start planning our own wedding. There might be a few hangups. They definitely will need time to adjust to the news. But I'm sure over time they'll come to accept us. They have to. Because I know it'll devastate James if he feels like he has to choose.

I wouldn't want him to choose anyway. They're his family. But then where would that leave me?

"Now that we finally have time to hang out, you can help me figure who the hussy is dating my dad.," Serena says.

That statement is like a bucket of cold water over my head. I must need my ears cleaned because that couldn't have been what she said. I was caught up in my own daydreams I missed out on what she was saying. "What do you mean?"

"Oh, I thought I told you. My mom found a receipt for a ring from Tiffany's in his car when she borrowed it last week and she said he told her he had something important to tell her and that's why he wanted everyone on this trip."

Even though I know the ring was for me, my heart pounds in my chest rapidly. They know. Or at least they think they do. But they think it's for someone else. "That

Although We Shouldn't

doesn't mean anything, though. Maybe he just wants everyone to come together again after the dust has cleared. You were just saying how you missed having family vacations."

"Yeah, but That doesn't discount that he bought a ring. No one buys a ring from Tifanny's unless it's serious. Let's be honest, if he should be with anyone, don't you think it would have been my mom?"

No.

He belongs to me. He's mine. My heart protests in my chest begging her to let it go. Let her dad be happy, no matter what. Because I know my best friend. If she's thinking this way now, she's thought about this for a while. She's like a dog with a bone once she wraps her mind around something. I love Serena. I do. But I can't help but feel selfish and wish for her to be more accepting of her dad being with someone else. Who knows? Maybe when she finds out it's me, she will like the idea more. Judging by the way she scrunches up her face, I'd take that as a no. There goes the smooth transition that everyone will accept us.

I can't help but think this is one more obstacle we have to overcome. A simple misunderstanding. But we all know what happens with misunderstandings, the same things as the best-laid plans. No matter how hard you try to explain things, someone always comes out hurt. "What if this girl makes your dad happy? More than he ever has been before. Would you be okay with it?" *Please say yes. Please say yes.*

"Are you kidding? The idea is too weird for me to think about. And what would he think he can do with a new woman? He already has two kids who are adults. And what? I'd get a baby brother or sister? Wouldn't that be weird?" She shows me another piece of clothing for my approval, but I can't focus from the buzzing in my ear. Her voice goes in and out as her words circle in my head. Would it be weird though? Serena loves kids. How could she not like the idea of having a baby sibling?

"Anyway, we still don't know who this woman is yet. We need more information.." My best friend yammers on completely obvious to the ticking time bomb going on inside my head. I hear my phone buzz on her dresser from an incoming text. I don't need to look to know who it is. I was supposed to meet James in an hour for a nightcap. Things couldn't have possibly taken such a nosedive.

There's still hope, a voice whispers in my head. I hold on to that for dear life and hope it's not wrong.

5

JAMES

"Everyone better be packed and loaded in the car in twenty minutes if they want to go on this trip." I yell up the stairs. All the kids have moved out of the house, including me, since I left the house to Elaine. But last night, everyone spent the night here, for old time's sake.

Serena said it brings back good memories now that we're going on a family trip again and that it's good luck to keep up the tradition. I don't know what she's hinting at but she's been directing looks at me all day. If I didn't know any better, I'd say she knew my secret with her best friend. However, Willow hasn't said a word since she came here. She's been peaking at me all day in between looking at Elaine. I wanted to pull her to the side and tell her that there was nothing to worry about. Yes, I get along with my ex-wife now, but all there is to it is healthy co-parenting.

A part of me feels like it's my fault if she has any doubts because I used to confide in her so much pre-divorce, so now she knows how I feel about Elaine—or felt. I thought it would make us grow closer together. Now?

Now I'm worried, especially since this is the second time

she's skirted past me without giving me one of our secret looks.

"I'm coming." Greyson yells as he barrels down the staircase. Greyson weighs two hundred and ten pounds of all muscles as a professional soccer player. But you would never know it with the sounds he makes as he walks. He sounds like an angry stampede of elephants. His gas smells that way too.

Willow walks past me again on her way to the bathroom, the tiny whiff of peaches and strawberries fills my senses. If I were a better man, I'd give her the space she wants, but fuck it. This whole trip is made so we can announce our relationship. I've never let her stew in her thoughts for long. I'm not about to let her waddle in it now. Making up my mind, I follow her down the hall, careful to make sure no one is paying attention, and follow her into the bathroom and close it shut. For added security, I lock the door.

"What?" She startles, wide eyes. Her blue eyes have a golden shimmer on them, and she has a deep pink gloss on her plump lips that I know tastes like pineapple. Her blonde hair is up in a sloppy bun and all I can think about right now, now that we're alone in the bathroom, is letting her hair down and finally giving her a deep kiss.

"You got ten seconds to tell me what's going on in that pretty head of yours before I take matters into my own hands and find out for myself," I growl against her ear. I see the nape of her hair rise up at my closeness and I smirk.

"Nothing's wrong," her throat swallows and my right-hand reaches out to grab it as my thumb slides down the column of her neck.

"Ten," I start counting. My mouth moves to her neck as my teeth scrape against her skin. My tongue darts on to moisten her sensitive neck as I pepper soft, hot kisses there shortly after.

"I'm serious. You're reading into things that aren't there," there's a slight stutter in her words as I reach my free hand down and unbutton her shorts.

"Nine," my index and middle fingers dip into her underwear and find her wet folds. My girl is ready for me even when she's lying. My finger gathers her slickness and glides up and down her entrance and pinch her clit.

Willow yelps and I release her throat to cover her mouth but keep my other hand on her hot pussy. "Careful, you wouldn't want to draw any attention this way. Not yet."

She relaxes and nods her head. I release her mouth and her skin flushes a bright red. "I'm tired. Serena had me up all night yammering. I barely got any sleep." The words seem believable because I know my daughter. She's a chatterbox. She can talk a man into pantyhose if she wants to. But even still. That isn't the reason why Willow has been acting skittish today. Looking into her eyes, I see the lie in there. The pleads to let this go. Not on my watch.

"Eight," I slip the two fingers into her and scissor them in her. She whimpers but is careful not to be too loud. My mouth goes back to her neck to give her attention and my other hand works its way under her white t-shirt to play with her nipples.

Fuck, my cock is pulsing in my jeans, begging to be released. Her juices coat down my hand and I sped up my ministrations. Our foreheads meet in the middle, and I groan. Her hand reaches out to my belt, but my stare freezes her in place. She knows that when I'm giving her my punishment, she isn't allowed to touch me.

That's my good girl.

"I can do this all day, sweetheart, so you better tell me what's wrong now. I'll keep them waiting if I have to." My brow raises in a challenge, and I feel the moment she decides to give in.

"Serena told me Elaine found the receipt for a ring in your car last week and how she's hoping to get back together with you." She whispers like she's afraid the moment she releases it from her lips. it'll come true.

Fat chance.

I don't love Elaine like I used to. Not like I love the beautiful woman standing in front of me begging me to erase her fears. Doesn't she see how much of her is a part of me. I wouldn't be risking the wrath of my family if I wasn't all in. My hand slides out of her as I frame my hands around her face.

"Look at me when I say this, please, I'm begging you.' I wait for her eyes to find mine and take a deep breath. "I am not in love with Elaine. I was, but there's another feisty, compassionate, sassy, downright hilarious, and tenderhearted woman who has the power to bring me to my knees with one look. And I'm fucking looking at her. Elaine may be a lot of things. The mother of my children. A friend—although it took us a while to get there. A great cook. But the most important thing is she is my past. And you are my now, tomorrow, and all my forevers. Where you go, I go. Always," I wait for her to finish our pact.

"And forever," a tear slides down her eye and I wipe it away with my thumb.

"Good girl, now turn around and bend over, so I can show you how much you belong to me." For a brief moment, I take great pleasure in the rapid flutter of her heartbeat in her neck at her excitement. I will never tire of her desire for me. The anticipation of the first moment of contact between us. I can practically feel my dick jump in my pants. Without waiting for her to move, I turn her toward the door, and she braces herself against it, as I pull her underwear and shorts down to her ankles and release my raging hard-on from my jeans, and slam into her.

Although We Shouldn't

We groan in pleasure as I smack her perky round ass. The sight of my red handprint on her ass makes me twitch inside her. Grabbing her hair, I release her hair from its hold and wrap it around my hand. Tugging it once, I lower myself to her ear and whisper, "Don't you ever question my love for you again."

She moves to nod her head, but I slam into her picking up a punishing past... In between smacks on her ass, I go around to her front and play with her clit. Her mouth opens in a silent scream from the building pressure. Her walls pulse around my dick sending bright stars to my eyes.

Fuucck.

I wish I had more time to play with her nipples some more. As it is, we already are on borrowed time. Again. Who knows how long my family will wait before they go searching for us. I need to hurry up.

My hand speeds up it pace in tandem with my strokes with I put a finger on her mouth. "Suck," I order her, and she opens her mouth complacently. I feel her tongue swirl around my finger as if she's sucking my goddamn cock and almost lost it.

I pinch her clit again and feel her legs start to buckle. A telltale sign she's close. A good thing to do because I'm not far behind.

"You are forever mine," I growl against her. "Mine." I slam into her. "Mine," I slam into her again and swirl my finger faster on her clit. She lets out a small cry in pleasure. In two more seconds, we both come together and sigh.

When she stands back up, and I slowly pull out; my release trickles down her leg. Her cheeks heat, but I'm not having that. It's proof of our love and I won't let her be embarrassed by it. "Later, when we both have time to calm down from the storm, I'll be filling you up so much, we won't know what to do with all. "

A grin covers her face bringing me my girl back. My hand reaches down to get a swipe of her moisture and I bring it to my mouth. It's a little of her and a lot of me. Who fucking cares. I moan and close my eyes. Opening them back up, I make sure I'm looking at her as I say, "The sweetest fucking pie I've ever tasted."

I readjust myself and button my pants back up before helping her get her clothes back on. If I wasn't being careful —or more careful than I should've been—I would've put her underwear in my pocket. But we don't need to be caught before we're ready. "Come on, baby girl. Let's go before they send the cavalry."

And it's a good thing we didn't leave a moment too soon because my ex was waiting at the door.

6

WILLOW

This is fucking torture. If I knew this was how the weekend was going to go, I would have just told everybody in a group text. All day I've had to keep my distance from James. Several times I found myself gravitating towards him, like some sort of home beacon. I was lucky no one really caught on before I forced myself to sit way on the other side. Elaine is by his side right now, chatting him up. Normally, if I wasn't in love with him, I wouldn't really be concerned. Serena and I would sneak away to see if there were any guys were around to have some fun of our own. But she's engaged now and I'm—stuck.

A big part of me wants to walk over to him and sneak away. To plant a big kiss right on his lips in front of everyone to get it over with. He wanted to wait for the perfect opportunity to bring it up though. Whatever that means. It's been three hours of pretending everything is normal and I can't take another second. My phone buzzes in my pocket and I reach down to take it out and read the text.

J: Relax.

I changed his name in my phone to just his letter, so I

wouldn't have the incriminating information in my phone if Serena got nosy and decided to go through. We're practically like sisters, so we use each other's phones all the time. Either to borrow it call or to stalk an exes socials, though we haven't done that in a long time.

J: I'm sorry It won't be much longer. I promise.

I sigh before glancing up at him from his spot by the barbecue. From where I'm sitting, I can see the pull between his brows and the phone in his hands. I decided to put my big girl pants on and suck it up. Besides, it won't be long, and I can take my spot by his side. I reach down in my shirt to pull the chain from around my neck that has the engagement ring on it.

Sighing I type, **It's fine. Not too long right?**

J: You sure?

I love him for worrying about me. He has been skirting around her advances and logically I know he can't really say anything to her that won't have her asking questions. Sue me for getting jealous though. What else is she supposed to think? To her, he's single. He hasn't brought anyone around the family, and Serena has hinted enough that her mom definitely wants him back.

Me: I'm sure. :)

I might regret this. I'll definitely regret it. The sun's UV rays break out of the clouds and shine extra hard down on us almost like it shining a light on where my heart lies. I walk away before I get any ideas about staking a claim and telling Elaina off. Peeling off my shirt and taking my shorts off—I changed clothes, thank you very much. I couldn't sit next to Serena and Greyson smelling like sex. My bathing suit is underneath, so I head over to the lake and jump in to cool off.

The water cools my skin as I sink in. Tipping my head back, I wet my hair and sink down. Down here, underneath

Although We Shouldn't

the water, nothing matters. I could spend hours down here and never worry about a thing. Unfortunately, I'm not a person who can hold my breath long and my lungs scream for air before I pop back up.

"Penny for your thoughts?" A voice says behind me.

Turning around in the water I see Greyson lounging on a chair by the edge. A mischievous smirk appears as he shakes his mousy brown hair. He gets his hair and facial features from his dad. They share the same sultry bedroom eyes and devil-may-care attitude. I almost wish I was into him and not his dad.

Almost.

But as luck would have it, my heart only beats for one man who is two times my junior.

I tip back to float on my back and put my arms behind my head. "No thoughts, just easy going from here." It's a lie. But it's not like I'm going to suddenly tell him how jealous I am that his mother has been coming onto his dad all day, and I can still feel his dad's dick in me from earlier before we left. No, thank you. Especially knowing that he has a huge crush on me. He slipped up one night when Serena and I picked him up from the bar one day. Greyson is a good guy.

A great guy even.

I just don't feel any sparks whenever I'm near him.

A sad twist of events, considering my life would be ten times easier if I felt anything for him.

When I'm with James, it's like fireworks erupt behind my eyes every time we kiss and the nerves beneath my skin buzzes. I can't feel the ground beneath my feet when he looks at me. His pensive blue eyes sweep over my entire body and give me a full-body shiver. I'm liquid goo. When Greyson looks at me, it feels like he's my brother. And as much as I love my real brother, Penn, I wouldn't kiss him.

Gross.

It's the same thing I feel with Greyson.

"Liar," Laughter bleeds into his teasing words. I hear him dip into the ocean and make ripples in the water as he makes his way to me. "I'll let you lie to me. For now, anyway."

I feel his body heat near me, and I sit up to swim backwards.

Playfully, I flick some water at him. "I thought this was supposed to be a fun trip. You know, family fun and all that jazz. Even though I'm crashing the family part." I laugh to ease away the tension that's suddenly there. It thick and messy and ruing the good vibes I was seeking.

He laughs as he shakes his black inky hair and splashes me with water. By the twinkle in his eye, it seems like he did that intentionally. "Nah," his shoulder hikes up. "I love family vacations and all. But Serena and I know the real reason why we're here."

My heart stutters in my chest and almost stops in its tracks. There's no way he could know the real reason his dad suggested this vacation. We were careful. Sure. We may have almost gotten caught when we pulled up together and gotten a quickie before everyone got her. But I'm almost certain no one saw us.

"Y-you do?" I wonder if this is what Edgar Allan Poe felt in a tell-tale heart. Almost on the brink of getting caught.

More of that easy laughter fell out of his lips as he rolled his eyes. "Yeah, Mom wants to get back together with my dad. She all but begged us to go along with it."

His voice tunnels out of my ears as I mentally freak out. No. No. No.

That's why Serena was all gung-ho about her parents getting back together. It was all Elaine's idea. There were a million things wrong with this scenario. And half of them were because my heart was screaming, "No, he's mine."

"I know, I know. It's gross to think about." He squeezes

Although We Shouldn't

his eyes close in disgust. "But if they want to who am I to get in the way of that."

I wheezed out painfully. My skin felt too tight on me, like it was a size too small. My chest felt [painfully tight like the air couldn't get out fast enough or the opening was too small for the air to pass through. My eyes found their way where Elaine was as she lounged on one of the lawn chairs that was conveniently placed in front of where James was grilling.

The waters suddenly didn't feel like the place I should be in. All my intrusive thoughts were saying it's best if I drown now because it'd be a safer death than causing this family any more distress than what they had been through.

This wasn't how this was supposed to go.

But stuck a thousand miles away from home, I had nowhere to escape.

"Hey, are you okay? You're looking a little pale." Blue eyes that resembled his dad's stared at me in concern. His hands went to my arms as they softly rubbed my arms. If I had been in better condition, I'd push him away. Set the record straight and tell him I was off limits—spoken for.

But as it was, my mind was on other pressing matters. Like how the strap of Elaine's bikini top was untied and if a little wind were to blow it would uncover her chest. How many times did James tell me she was his past? Too many to count. This didn't feel like the past though. No. It felt very much like his present.

And what was I doing letting her get away with this? I couldn't stake my claim on him just yet. however, I didn't have to make it easy for her either.

With my mind set, I started swimming back to shore, with my sights set on my man. A cold, wet hand stopped me as he pulled me to his front. "Wait, I'm sorry—I just—let me start over." He inhaled a deep breath before looking in my eyes.

No.

Oh my god no.

Something about the seriousness set in his eyes. The way they gentled before they casted an iridescent sheen told me this was like watching a car crash waiting to happen. He laughed nervously before grabbing a hold of my hand. "I wanted to tell you this since last summer. It's so silly. I don't know why I'm nervous."

I did. It was the same reason why I felt hot all over, thinking about anyone else with his father other than me. The same reason why I knew I couldn't wait any longer to finally tell everyone James and I were together. I was busting at the seams waiting to do it. The same reason why I recognized it in Greyson is because I felt it too. Just not for him—love.

And I couldn't stand for one more heartbreak this weekend.

So, I cut him off. "Don't say it." I gave him a sad smile. "Please don't say it."

His eyes questioned me with a confused smile. "You don't even know what I'm going to say yet."

My eyes closed in pain. Not for me. But for him. Because I didn't deserve this poor guy's heart. He should give it to someone else. Someone who can love him the same way.

"I do," wetness dampened my cheeks. Tears. I was crying, because life wasn't fair. Why would it let good people fall in love only for it to be unrequited? Unappreciated. Love deserves to be appreciated and reciprocated, because when it's half full and nowhere for it to go, it festers in the heart and turns into resentment. If the person doesn't learn to let it go, it can destroy the strongest organ in your body—your heart. "I'm telling you I'm not the one."

"You are," his words were desperate and needy in the most heartbreakingly painful way. I remember feeling that

Although We Shouldn't

way the summer I got my heart broken and cried my eyes out with Serena at Tony's. I only hoped this wouldn't hurt him as much as I had hurt then.

"No," I said sadly. "I'm not."

"How do you know? You haven't even given us a chance yet?" "Trust me, okay? I'm all wrong for you."

"My heart says you're wrong, just please," He grabbed my face and landed his lips on mine. And though they were soft and pliant, they were all wrong. Because these weren't the lips I wanted. I pushed him off me with little force and because he wasn't expecting that he stumbled back slightly, almost falling backward before he righted himself.

Hurt crested on his face before he looked me in the eye. "There's someone else isn't there?" His throat bobbed on a slow swallow, like what he was about to say next was painful, but he had to say it. He looked dejected and heartbroken. And a little mad. "J, right?" He asked.

I glanced up at him, surprised. I didn't know whether I should lie to protect the truth from him a little bit longer or if I should put him out of his misery. The seconds ticked by like little mini bombs setting off. I desperately looked for a way out. Out of this conversation. Out of this trip. Out of the never-ending obstacles that screamed this trip was a mistake. So many glaring signs beamed at me telling me this was never going to end well and me and James were only fooling ourselves.

"Don't bother denying it. I read one of your messages while you were in the water." He tilted his chin up defiantly. His shoulders loosened on an exhale. "I thought, I thought, if I proved to you that you had other options, that I was the better choice…" his voice drifted off choppily. He was barely holding himself together.

My heart hurt for him.

Truly, it did.

I just didn't know how to make it any better.

"Maybe I convinced myself it wasn't too late. I wasn't that drunk that night I confessed my feelings for you, you know."

My eyes met his and saw the sincerity bleeding through. His eyes were begging me to see him. And I did. Not in the way he wanted me to, but I saw this perfectly great guy asking to be loved. He was asking the wrong person, though. "So, why did you play if off the next day?" I wasn't sure the answer mattered. Because at the end of the day, I wasn't going to magically reciprocate his feelings. It left me confused. Twisted in this never ending incestial web of lies and secrets and despair.

The next morning, he woke up and played it off like he couldn't even remember he got home. He razzed me and Serena for being goody two shoes and how we never got out and lived. He bragged about the numbers he pulled from girls and said he was going to call it a day and stay in. He never brought anything up again. I was so sure that he was delirious—drunk—and had mistaken the person who he was talking to. I was relieved. Because I couldn't handle holding his heart in my hands. Even if it was a tiny crush.

Serena mocked me saying how weird it'd be if I ended up with her brother. She practically all but admitted she was glad I never had feelings for her brother, because I was family to her. At the time, me and James had found our footing in our relationship, and I was on cloud nine. I never felt bad about being called family by them. I embraced it. They were like my family too. But coming from her mouth right then, felt like charred coal in my mouth. Brittle and unrelenting.

"I was embarrassed. Your face turned pale white, kind of like how it was a minute ago. I told myself if I gave you time to come to terms with how I felt. If I gave you space to fall in love with me too, I could bring it up again. I started inserting

Although We Shouldn't

myself into your life more. If you needed help, I was there. Help with interviews, I was there for you. Only, you never once said anything. Not even a hint of attraction. I thought you were shy."

I couldn't bear to hear any more words coming out of his mouth. All those moments he was talking about barreled through me like a self-deprecating montage, mocking me at how blind I've been. Too wrapped in my own feelings and secrecy to see anything else. Anyone else. I wonder what else I've been blind to. I itch to look over at Elaine again, to see the details I may have missed over time. I didn't want to give myself away.

Not when someone else was demanding my attention.

"You were always so reserved after your breakup. I just thought you needed time to heal and then I could show you love could be a beautiful thing."

"I'm so sorry," it was a jagged whisper on my tongue. Because never in a million years had I wanted to hurt him. Yes, he was always there for me, but I had always thought it was because he was like a brother to me. I hated myself a little right then for being the one to break his heart. I didn't see a way out of it.

He wanted my heart.

But I gave it to someone else.

"I figured," his voice was raspy, caught on shaky, water exhale. His teeth ground together as he held his emotions in.

It was funny because right then it feels like I needed air. Because the air around grew stale and thick, wrapping around my lungs and squeezing tight. We were outside surrounded by fresh air and it wasn't enough. I didn't know where I was going as I walked around him with my head down. I knew I couldn't stand here any longer.

"If I had spoken up sooner, would it have made a difference?" He said at my back.

I turned my head to meet his eyes once more. I didn't have to say anything. I felt the truth of it all written all over me. Weighing me down like a hundred-pound weight. No matter what he would have done, I couldn't have returned his feelings. I saw the minute he saw that truth too. A tear finally broke free before he stormed off ahead of me.

"Hey, where ya going, bud?" James asked as he put his hands on his son's shoulder.

Greyson shook him off. "I just need some space for a few minutes."

James's brow pulled down on his forehead in concern. He looked over at me for help. I shook my head as I got out of the water and walked over to him.

"What happened?" Elaine asked walking over to us.

James and Elaine shared a look. A look they've shared many times before. Years of trust were built between them. A history. I wanted to laugh at that word. Everything seemed to be mocking me today. They looked every bit the family as they were. And here I was, the interloper.

"He's just being a guy," I mumbled. The lie rolled bitter off my tongue.

They looked at me in confusion.

Suddenly, I too needed space.

Only for a moment.

7

JAMES

Darkness coated the night as everyone was asleep in their rooms. Everyone except me. Greyson finally came back after an hour, nonchalant and evasive. Elaine had tried to get him to open up earlier and like before he brushed her off claiming it was nothing. He had told us he needed to clear his head. Get in some nature and be alone. I did not doubt the alone part. He was always a lone wolf when something bothered him. I wish I knew what it was that was bothering him. I remember the days he would tell me anything. No detail was too little for him to tell me. And now, with this one thing, it's like pulling teeth.

He made a million promises he was fine. But my intuition knew he was lying. I also had a feeling it was about the other guest who had yet to return. Willow.

That was my other suspicion.

Something was said between them. Something that caused a rift between them. Because anytime she was brought up, Grey got up and left. We were all confused. And I was stuck. Unsure how to mend the break in the flow of our lives. I needed to talk to Willow. See where her head's at and maybe pull some answers out of her.

If we were to announce our relationship and go public, we couldn't hide from each other anymore. That means when something is on her mind, she turns to me first before trying to figure it out on her own. Slipping on my boots, I head out the door without tying them,

It was time I find my girl and bring her back to me. Carefully, so the door wouldn't slam and wake everyone up, I pulled it closed behind me.

Nothing but silence greeted me as I edged into the woods. My feet crunched on the ground as I stopped on stray twigs and leaves. My mind raced with a million thoughts. I followed the air around me, feeling like it was a guiding force, bringing me closer to my destination.

After walking about a mile in, I find my girl at a creek underneath a Willow tree. How fitting to find her by her namesake.

"Hey, what are you doing all the way out here?" My voice is careful and quiet, so I won't scare her.

She barely turns around to answer me. Her face tipped toward the moon. "Everything is so peaceful out here. Sometimes, I forget how trivial things can be when I think of us in terms of space and time." Her arms wrap around herself like she's trying to ward off bad energy.

I could never keep myself from her long, so I stood behind her and let my heat seep into her bones as a second layer of protection. Her silent sentry.

"Have you ever wanted to just go away and never come back?" Her words freeze the blood in my veins. Between this and my son acting weird, I didn't know which way was up.

My words were careful. "What happened?"

"Greyson thinks he loves me." At her words, she turned around and searched my eyes. I laid everything out for her to

Although We Shouldn't

see. I was completely exposed, vulnerable. I'd do this a million times over if it eased her fears. They were the loudest things in the air around us.

I love you. I need you. See me. See how gone I am without you. Be here with me.

"Did he tell you that?" My heart thumped in my chest. A frantic desperate beat.

She nods.

"So that's what that was about earlier? Why he had stormed off?" It made sense. The pieces were slowly coming together. I needed to see the rest of the picture, though, to see how it fit in with her earlier question.

"Yeah. He knows there's someone else—not you in particular. But that I'm seeing someone else." Her eyes are two glistening gems as they beg me to take the heaviness out of her heart. She never has to ask me for anything. I would give her my own heart if it meant she could live another day. I gather her in my arms and tip her head up, so our eyes can meet. She meets me halfway and kisses me with a force I didn't know I was longing for. I feel our souls connect in this silent duel to mold against each other. To become one. My hands pull her closer to me. This is what I needed. Reassurance. I couldn't stand it if she decided this was too much for her. That the plights of our relationship were something she couldn't withstand.

"How can he not love you?" I ask as we separate. I put her hand on my chest and let her feel my heart thump in an attempt to bleed in her hands. Feel how my heart beats for her and her alone. "You are the moon and the stars in the nighttime sky. You shine where you go, and you don't even know it. You are the blades of grass on a springtime day. You are the slow waves in the ocean crashing into the shore as it meets land. You are the clouds on a sunny day providing shade. You are every important little detail that makes a day the best one anyone has ever had—the best I have ever had. What's not to love about you?" She choked on a sob, and I pulled her closer, hoping to absorb all her pain. I knew my girl was hurting for my son. For his breaking heart and the unknowing hand, she played in it.

She was everything good in this world and tried to be everything for everyone in a way she knew how. But this? She couldn't give this to him. And she hated herself for it. I wish she knew that nothing she did or could ever do would tarnish the light that's inside of her. Nothing can make her beautiful soul ugly, damaged.

She sniffles, wiping more tears away from her gorgeous sea-blue eyes. "Do you ever think about it?"

There are a lot of things I think about. Like the ramifications our actions will hold to our future, if we can stand the test of time, how I got so lucky to be with such an amazing woman. "Think about what, doll face?" My fingers wisp over her face, not being able to not touch her for longer than a minute. I'm greedy with my time with her.

"About how many hearts will break once we tell them?" Her voice was beautifully haunting as she stared at a distant spot over my shoulder. I guess she can't face me as she admits the hard truth. Up until now I couldn't either. "They'll be disappointed you know, hurt, betrayed. The moment Greyson told me how he felt, I started looking at the tiny details that I somehow missed. And everything sharpened to a degree that I can't believe I missed. The way Elaine has been so friendly towards you. How she sought out every opportunity to be near you. You can't tell me you missed that."

She's right. I thought Elaine and I had moved past our history. Our love that we once had. All day I've had to step back from her several times. I had chalked it up to her being comfortable. I guess I was avoiding having to have a difficult

Although We Shouldn't

conversation before it was too soon. This weekend was supposed to give everyone a safe place to enjoy good times before we told them. To soften the blow. But it's been one shit storm after another.

"Right," Willow swallows as she blows out an agitated breath.

"So, what do you want to do?" It seems no matter which direction I go in, my decision will affect someone. Not only will Elaine be hurt, but my son will be too. Everyone always says to follow your heart. It's easier said than done when you have nothing to lose. I love Willow. How can she expect me to give her up? Not even the strongest man can let go of the most beautiful thing in the world. She's become my eighth wonder of the world. At the same time, I couldn't lose my family either.

She leans her head against my chest and admits, "I want time to stop for a second, so I can think."

Slowly, I edge us down to the bank of the woods and lay her on the ground. She stares up at me, her blue orbs shimmering in the night, a beacon to my soul. Blonde wisps of her hair tangle in the grass and cover her face. I peel them back, desperate to see the parts of her she keeps hidden from the world. "Then let's go back in time."

Her laughter becomes music with the sounds of nature. "How are we going to do that?" A hint of a smile peeks on her face, open curiosity in her eyes.

"Do you know when I first knew I loved you?" I ask. I'm not sure I ever told her this. I know when I first told her I loved her. I was a mumbling fool, nervous to open my heart up again after it had been pulverized in the divorce.

Her nose scrunches, which makes her dimples even more pronounced. She shakes her head.

"We were going for a drive out of town last spring because you had this chocolate smoothie craving. And you couldn't wait for the weekend because you said work had been a bitch." I remember it like it was yesterday. A moment I will take with me to my grave.

"And a girl needs a pick me up when life is bitchin'." She laughs remembering what she told me.

"I remember thinking, what the hell did I sign up for because I was up to my neck in invoices for car repairs because a certain someone had come into my job almost every day for a quickie." My eyes playfully glare at her.

Another chuckle slips free. The tension in her brows slowly dissipates.

"What was I doing? I was a forty-two year-old man, who had bills to pay and a company to keep afloat. And here this young twenty-six-year-old was asking me to slip away from my adult responsibilities for a pick me up." I chuckle to myself remembering how lost I felt. How out of my depth I felt. I hadn't wanted to let her down, but I also felt like my hands were tied.

If anything were to happen to my company because I let little things slip away, then what was I going to do when I lost it. It seemed an impossible task then. Before I had hired a manager full time to help with the administrative things.

"I had to ask Manny at the shop to cover for me for the rest of the day with the promise he could take off half a day that weekend. And who would give up that offer?" He had all but rushed me out of my chair, telling me to take all the time I needed.

"I didn't know that. I thought you had finished things early at your job," she muses. Her fingers dart toward my face. Tracing the lines around the edges and smoothing out the hard lines from years of experience and hard work had formed. It became her favorite thing to do when we would lay awake all night.

"I would do anything for you. Don't you know that by

Although We Shouldn't

now? What was I going to do? Let you spiral alone when I could be there for you."

"The best man," her voice a whisper as she waits for the next part in the story.

Slowly, I tell her all about that day as the crickets chirp into the night.

Last Spring

"Boss, we got another call for faulty brake pads. The owners want to know if we can fix it today if they tow it in." He leans against the wall as he glances at the mountain of paperwork on my desk. He whistles, raising his brows. "Although, I'm guessing from the looks of things, you have other things to worry about."

I sigh, dropping the pencil in my hand. I learned the hard way not to do invoice bookkeeping by pen. Too many mistakes can be made. Especially if I was trying to rush through them like I was now. I usually did the week's invoices during my lunch time, but Willow had shown up every day this week, looking like a walking siren and said she was feeling dangerous and decided an afternoon quickie was in order.

God knew I was a weak man for my biggest temptation.

I had put the papers away every time and dug into the soft, smooth flesh of her body and lost myself into her. Time after time again.

Now I had a mountain of invoices to catch up on. People to call to see when they can make their payments to be able to balance my books by the end of the month. I didn't want to haggle another customer for last minute walk ins. My business as an auto mechanic show had gotten so busy, busier than I'd ever imagined, thanks to hiring the right mechanics and paying them above their pay grade, which meant, few and far between, had we allowed walk-ins.

"Do we have the space available for the car to come in?" I asked. If I worked a little later, I could fit the repair in and have it ready by the morning. I've been putting in more time lately to have a small nest egg saved up. Emergencies always happened in my life, like last month when the water pipe burst in my apartment, and I had to pay a plumber to fix it if I didn't want my place to drown.

He hummed as he thought about it. "We might if the Sheppard's car is fixed soon enough. Every other port is filled with new repair orders."

We shared the same dubious looks with one another. The Sheppards paid us top dollar to fix their son's car. She crashed it into a pole after a late night of binge drinking. I hope they won't give the car back to him. He's a menace on the road, and someday he'll cost someone their life. But they're rich society people. They had no clue about the societal obligations they were supposed to have, nor did they care. Regardless, it would take time to fix everything wrong with the car. We thought it was just cosmetic damage. But the kid had also blew out the engine from placing an engine in it that was fit for a race car when his car was built for a smaller engine. That was when we decided to do a full checkup on the car. Aside from the blown engine, the gas valve needed to be repaired because he used the wrong gas, and the transmission was acting funny due aggressively street racing.

It was safe to say that there wouldn't be any space to fix whoever wanted their brake pads fixed.

"Got it, boss. I'll let them know that we're booked up right

Although We Shouldn't

now and to recommend them to a nearby shop they can go to. Let me know if you need anything." He tapped the door twice before leaving to hand the customer. Manny was a great employee. He handled the phone calls and was also one of the best mechanics. He was scrappy with his hands and resourceful when the time came for it. He was half the reason the place was doing so well.

I didn't blink an eye at turning the customer away. When I first started my business, I accepted anyone and everyone, desperate to hit the ground running. Now, we were doing exceptionally well and could afford to turn people away. Heck, it ended up working out for us anyway because the other shops did the same for us when they were busy. This town was a community for the small-town folks. It was the biggest reason why I decided to quit my finance job.

Turning back to my paperwork, I pick up another invoice and was about to get back to work when my cell phone rings. I sigh, roughing the stubble on my face aggressively. I am never going to get anywhere with all these interruptions. But it is the ringtone I never ignored.

Willow. The brightest spot of my day.

Picking it up, I hit answer. "Hey beautiful," the words tumbled from my mouth freely. I look around to make sure no one was listening. Not that I was ashamed of her. But our relationship was a very new and unorthodox. We liked having our privacy to find our way into things. It also helped the fact that we were keeping it well hidden from everyone.

"I'm having the worst day." She moans into the phone. Car horns blaze through her end of the phone from wherever she is.

"Where are you?" My ears strain to pick up more clues about her whereabouts but could hear nothing else. I swear to God if she was driving while on the phone, I'd have to have another talk with her about the dangers of being on the phone while driving. It's bad enough that Serena doesn't listen to my words of caution.

"Relax, I'm pulled over by my job." I could practically hear her eyes rolling in her head. So much sass my girl had. I love it. But not for this. I don't care how old I sound to her, her safety will always come first to me.

"Okay, good," I blow out a relieved breath. "So, what's up doll face, why are you having a bad day." My eyes skim over the invoice, hoping to multitask while still being on the phone. I usually gave her my undivided attention, but again, responsibilities.

"Not a bad day babe. The *worst* day." She emphasized the word worst.

"Okay, why is it the worst day?"

"Because, I woke up late because Serena kept up all night with the disgusting sex sounds she was making with this new guy she's seeing,"

Okay, gross. I did not need to know about my daughter's sex life.

"And that made me late for work, so I was speeding on the road, which meant I got pulled over and ticketed. I even tried to flirt my way out of the ticket like Serena taught me how. Don't tell her I told you that though. You aren't supposed to know she's been speeding. Anyway, after receiving a forty-dollar ticket, which made me even later, I arrive to work and Josh, the douchebag, stole credit for my work–AGAIN, and got the raise I'd been vying for. It's bullshit."

"First, gross. I didn't need to know that about my daughter and whoever she's dating. Second, I'm sorry about your ticket. Do you need to borrow money? I know your job doesn't pay you that well yet?"

"No, no. It's fine. I can pay it. Thanks for offering."

"Anytime. Josh is a—what did you call him?" I scratch my

Although We Shouldn't

head trying to remember which slang term she used to call him. There are so many these days I can't keep up.

"Douche canoe," she chuckles as a sniffle slips through, letting me know she's crying. My heart clamors in my chest. I could never handle a girl's tears. The minute Serena mastered the art of crying on command, I knew I was a sucker. Hearing this girl, this *woman*, I've begun to care for beyond my wildest expectations, cry is worse ten times over.

"Right, he's a douche canoe. Swim down the river and lose the paddle all the way." I say with earnest. Screw him for fucking over my girl. Willow works hard at her job as a Marketing Specialist. We stayed up all night one day creating the perfect pitch to ask her boss for the job promotion to Marketing Manager. To see all the fruits of her labor get passed off to someone else is a huge blow, even for me. I wanted this for her as much as she did.

"God, you're so corny." More of her easy laughter slips out of her mouth.

My heart heats in my chest hearing her laugh. I think it's the best thing about Willow, how easily she laughs at life. She can be the most serious person in the room. But she'll also be the first person to laugh or to get you to laugh. It's her most endearing character. She's full of life, and her infectious energy transferred over to me when we started hanging out. "Well, only for you, baby girl. Only for you."

After a couple of minutes of silence over the phone. Minutes of us just listening to each other breathe and take in life she exhales as her tears come to a stop. "I could really go for a pick me up right about now."

"What about work?" I ask, squinting at the red numbers on the next invoice. Damn, if I'm late on another payment that will set us behind a couple hundred of bucks.

"What about work? Why go back to a job that undervalues me? I'm this rock-ass marketer that brings in all the sales and have nothing to show for it. And you want to know why?" she huffs over the phone. I guess she got her second wind already.

"Why, baby girl?"

"Because they suck monkey balls, that's why."

I let loose a deep belly laugh as I leaned back in my chair. This girl has got a mouth on her. It may not always be colorful, but it is creative. "Monkey balls?"

"Yes. Big. Huge. Hairy. Smells like farts monkey balls."

"Well, I'm sure they'd miss you even more if you left work. Even after sucking all those balls." There's a sentence I never thought I'd be saying.

"Who cares? I need this, James. Please. Don't argue with me on this." She sighs. I hear some rustling around on her end. I guess she was getting her things together or moving around. I honestly can't tell at this point.

"You don't need my permission. Just erring on the side of caution is all." I glance at the time on my watch noting the time. If I delay anymore, I'll be late on working on Mr. Peterman's car horn. Although, he really didn't need to bring it to me overnight to fix it. It all worked out though, because I haven't started on it yet. "Hey, listen, Willow, I really need to get started on some things, but I'll talk to you later okay?"

Silence.

She doesn't say a word.

I glance at the phone to see if we disconnected. *Nope*. The call is still on.

"Willow?" I ask.

"I'm here. I was hoping you could come with me." Sorrow seeps into her words, pulling on my heartstrings.

"You know I'd love to. But I have so much to do. You can ask Manny if you want. Matter of fact don't ask Manny. He's busy too." I cringe. It sounds like I'm brushing her off when I'm really not.

Although We Shouldn't

"Please," it a quiet plea whispered on the phone. "I really want to see you."

"I thought you wanted a chocolate smoothie." I counter, putting a lightness in my tone.

"I do. But I also need you." Damn her for knowing just what to say to make me reconsider everything.

"Fine. Give me an hour to finish some stuff up and I'll pick you." I conceded. I'll see if Manny can help out. At this rate, I'd offer him anything in return. Anything to put a smile on my girl's face. *Damn.* That never gets old. Even thinking about it puts a smile on my face.

"Thank you thank you thank you," Willow gushes over the phone.

"It had better be worth the drive we're going to have to take in the middle of the day," It's a tease rolling off my tongue. I'm already getting up and heading over to the door to start on Peterman's horn. It should take me thirty minutes top, leaving me fifteen minutes to go home and shower and another fifteen to pick her up.

"Trust me it is. A girl needs a pick me up when life gets bitchin."

I chuckle once more. "Okay, fair point. One hour. And meet me at our spot."

"One hour," she promises and hangs up.

One problem down.

Now I need to see about a guy doing some basic math.

8

JAMES

Exactly one hour later and my car is pulling up to our spot, at a nature park by the pond on the far right side. There she is in a white t-shirt and a pair of cut-off jeans with the bottoms rolled up on her ankle. Her wheat blonde hair is left out and she has on white sneakers with one of my plaid shirts that she's stolen tied around her hips. Even with no makeup on she takes my breath away.

I pull up next to her and roll my window down. "All that beauty ain't fair, darling. What's an old man to do when you give him a heart attack?"

She whips around at the sound of my voice and her entire face lights up. She speeds over to me, her hair blowing in the wind. She reminds me of a pixie floating in the sky. I open my door and brace myself for her to throw herself at me. Closing the door behind me as I get out, I open my arms. I only have about a second before she lands with an impact. "There's my girl." I say softly into her hair. Her arms and legs wrap around me, encasing me in her peach and spice scent.

I remember when she first spent the night. The scent was everywhere in my apartment. I couldn't escape it for days after. Every hint of her was everywhere for me to find. Following me. Infecting me and my senses with her girly deliciousness.

"You came," her face tips up to me and my heart stops. I never want to be without her smile again. I love her laugh, but her smile can rival even the Mona Lisa. I'd start a thousand wars just to be able to keep her smiling.

"Of course, I came. Where else would I be?" I ask as I walk her over to her side of the car.

She shrugs, swinging her hands between us and latching onto mine. "You sounded busy when I called."

"I'm never too busy for you, don't you know that?" And I mean it too. Things might not always be perfect between us, but anytime she needs me, I find myself looking for ways to get to her.

Her cheeks heat at my words. My fingers brush over her cheek. She leans back on the door and gazes up at me. "Hi," the words are shy and playful.

"Hi," I smile. I look around me to make sure no one is nearby. This park may be empty most times, due to it just being open pasture and trails, but sometimes the occasional hiker walks along these trails. And it is still daylight out, so I have to be careful when I give her public displays of affection —like now. My hand grabs a hold of her chin and her eyes close, waiting for contact. I won't let her wait long before my lips meet hers. A moan slips free, and her hand reaches out for my shirt, grabbing onto me.

My free hand lands on the car above her head. Our kiss isn't rushed or fast. We take our time exploring each other. She surprises me when she slips on a little tongue and duels with mine. I growl, pressing into her more. Showing her how much my body appreciates this new development between us.

She giggles, breaking contact and panting for air. But her

Although We Shouldn't

cheeks are still as rosy as ever and there's an impish sparkle in her eye. "I've been waiting to do that forever."

"Forever huh?" I open the door and help her in my truck. When she's all situated, I close the door and hurry to my side.

"Yes, I felt like I'd die if I couldn't get my hands on you for another minute," she answers once I'm in.

I start the car. At a later time, a time when I'm cooled off and my dick is begging me to set him free from my pants, I'll ruminate why I'm not scared to hear the words forever slipping from her mouth. I should be running for the hills and warning her it's too early to say anything like that. We've only been dating for six months. But right now, I'll just enjoy her company.

"Only your hands?" More teases and easy laughter.

Her cheeks turn a deeper shade of red, which causes me to look over at her and raise my brows. "Oh Miss Stanton, please do tell me all those wicked thoughts that caused to turn a pretty shade of red." My voice turns coarse and thick, filled with need. We've never gone there before. I don't want to pressure her into anything too soon. We're taking it slow for now. Only a couple of kisses or fevered touches. It's good enough for me for now. But damn, the girl can turn me on like no other.

Her hands cover her face, hiding from me. "And other things," she relents.

"Do tell, I'd love to know what has you so dripping wet I can smell your arousal from here." Testing the waters, my hand slips to her parted thighs and I rest it there as my thumb softly smooths over her through her jeans. When she doesn't immediately turn me away, I get a little braver and go an inch higher.

Her breathing turns heavy as her head turns to me. Her blue eyes turn black with need. But I'm not making any moves until she says it's okay with her mouth. We still have a ways to go, but we're on a busy part of the highway, so I remove my hand and venture onto a safer topic.

"So, tell me about this smoothie craving you have."

I can't tell if she's grateful for the subject change or disappointed. But I know I'm relieved.

I couldn't take another second without feeling like I'm going to bust.

Once she has her smoothie in hand and we're parked off in a wooded area in a nearby town that's just ten miles out, I get the trunk of my car ready for our usual hangouts. Two thick blankets, two pillows, and twinkling lights. The twinkling lights were her idea one night after she saw how worried I was about my headlights drawing too much attention. She said fairy lights—as she called them—were a better alternative, that way we weren't completely in the dark and weren't drawing too much attention.

"Here. Try some," She dips her spoon into her smoothie and offers it to me to taste.

I look at her questioningly before pushing her hand away. "No, this was for you. So, your day is a little less bitchin."

Her shoulders shake in silent laughter. "It's okay, I want you to try it." She offers it back to me.

My mouth opens and she plops the spoon in my mouth. Instantly, I'm hit with a dose of chocolatey goodness and a hint of peanut butter and nutmeg. The flavor explodes in my mouth, and I moan in appreciation. "You're right. This is good."

She beams at the compliment like she's the one who made it. "Told you."

She finishes the last of her smoothie and places it across from her. "Did I ever thank you for coming with me?"

Although We Shouldn't

"About a thousand times. But I already told you, it's no big deal." I scoop her in my arms and lie down with her. Her body fits into mine like the missing puzzle piece. We shouldn't work so well together, but we balance each other out. When I'm too serious she draws the silliness out of me and when she's worked up. I calm her down.

I feel her fingers on my face, tracing the outlines and ridges on my face. The underside of her hand smooths over my stubble.

"What are you doing?" I ask her. Her face is directly hanging over mine.

"Tracing the patterns of my heart." She said so confidently and sweetly.

There she goes again saying things that should scare me, but it doesn't. In fact, my heart thump, thump, thumps in my chest in a silent plea, saying pick me, choose me. My right hand follows suit and gently glides along her back.

"Did you have a busy day today?" She asks. Her brows pull thoughtfully. What drew me to her initially was her kind heart. We found ourselves running into each other a lot after that first night we bumped into each other in the middle of the night, her with her hot chocolate and me with a cup of Jameson. Over time, I would switch to coffee. Instead, basking in the comfort of another person who would listen. Offering up the chance for me to purge the weight on my shoulders. Much like she is now.

If I tell her the truth, she'll blame herself for pulling me away. She'll feel bad about pressuring me into leaving work. When I could never say no to her, which isn't her fault at all. So, I do the only thing to avoid hurting her feelings, just this once, and lie. "No, my day wasn't busy at all." I pressed a soft kiss on her hand, and it immediately curled around my face. Her touch was soft and gentle, and I wondered how long before I became completely addicted to the type of attention that she was giving me.

She laid back down, leaving her hand protectively on the side of my face. "Then it all worked out perfectly then." She sighed in contentment.

"What are you going to do about work?" I asked her. I didn't want to dampen her mood. We had enjoyed a nice drive and a nice chocolate smoothie. She was a lot more relaxed than when I first picked her up. A part of me, though, couldn't help but worry about the reason why we're here. I wanted to ensure she was on a good path and happy with her choices.

I turned my head to glance down at her when she didn't immediately answer. She was gnawing on her lips. Something she did when something was weighing on her mind.

"I was thinking about quitting," she admits softly, timidly —almost as if she's afraid of my reaction. Her eyes shoot up to mine, searching for my reaction. The soft hues of green in them brightens her eyes the longer she looks at me. As she holds her breath for my response, I realize she isn't afraid of my reaction. She values my opinion.

The magnitude of this revelation weighs on me and it's something I'll carry with honor.

Carefully, I chose my words. "If you quit, then what would you do? How will you have money?" My job isn't to dissuade her from her choices. I'm not her father. Thank fuck for that. But to allow her thoughts to process and allow her to make her own decisions.

"I was thinking of starting my own business for a while," her hands hold mine and I squeeze her hand gently in support.

"Oh yeah? What would you do?"

Excitement shoots up her spine, lifting her up from my arms and she turns to face me. "Okay, I was thinking I could

Although We Shouldn't

open up a social media company. It's practically what I do at work, only at a more niche scale. I could spread the word online and develop a small clientele to start off. You know, to get my feet wet."

I could see her doing so well with this. My little social butterfly. She was so headstrong, that once she put her mind to something, she'd eventually see it through. I saw it many times when she came across a new venture. When she wanted to learn how to skate last winter and was at the ice rink almost every day before she mastered the basics. When she decided she'd be a bartender before she landed her marketing job. She came home every night with tons of tips. It was like she had the Midas touch. Everything she touched turned out to be successful. \

There's no doubt in my mind she'll be successful with this new business.

"I can see you doing that. Landing new clients and being this badass media mogul babe." My smile lifted my face, and I sat up to face her fully.

"Yeah?" Her eyes sparkle in excitement. "And I wouldn't fully quit my job until I have a large enough nest egg and at least three clients landed. I know I have to figure a lot out about the business side of things. But I have time before I even land my first contracted job. That way I can do things right." Her hands flap about as she explains her plans.

I'm amazed at this woman before me.

How animated she is with everything she wants to do. She has so much passion and drive. I'm attracted to everything about her. Never in a million years did I think I'd get this lucky. Not twice. Being in love twice is a gambler's game.

Whoa.

Love?

Now, that I stop and think about it. The signs are all there. I am completely taken with Willow Stanton. The bright-eyed, compassionate, sexy as hell, and all-around maddening woman. She drives me fucking crazy in the best of ways and I look forward to every day we get to spend together.

There's no doubt about it now. And now that I know, there's nothing for me to do but enjoy the ride. I smile at her, brushing an errant strand of hair out of her face and look into two gorgeous pools of blue. My Willow. My everything.

She smiles quizzically at me. "What's so funny?" Her head tilts to the side.

I shake my head and my smile spreads bigger. "Nothing, darling."

"Tell me."

"I bet you already have a name for this company that you haven't even started yet, don't you?" I can bet my top dollar she does. My girl doesn't do anything halfway.

She grins like a kid with a secret. "Through The Willow Tree Media" Her dimples make an appearance again, making me a goner. "You think it's a bad name don't you."

"Absolutely not. And if I didn't know any better, I'd say people will adore the name as much as I adore the owner."

She beams under my praise and kisses me feverishly. I grab her head and pull her down on me. "You really think so?" She asks.

"Honey, there's not a day where I don't believe in you. Go rock the media world and I will be right there with you."

"Promise?" she held out her pinky finger and I linked mine with hers.

"Promise."

9
WILLOW

"You knew you loved me then?" I ask in wonder. My heart pounds erratically in my chest. I love hearing our story play back in his perspective, seeing how he viewed me in our early dating stage. My eyes catch his and I see nothing but sincerity in his eyes.

"I think I always knew how I felt about you but was too scared to admit it until then." His gruff voice sends shivers down my spine. I feel my lady bits get tingly and wet.

"Tell me more," I demand. I don't know what it is, whether it's the anticipation of tomorrow when we tell everyone our news or the conversation with Greyson, but everything in me is on fire tonight. I'm itching at the skin to be with him. Forever this time.

No reservations. No secrets.

Just eternally his.

"What do you want to know?" he asks patiently.

"What about the first time you knew you liked me as more than Serena's friend."

"You mean more than just my daughter's best friend?" His brows rise, knowing the reason why I avoided phrasing it that way. I've always been the one to shy away from pointing out the obvious taboo nature of our relationship. It makes us feel dirty and perverse when we are anything but.

"Yes, that."

"That's an easy one." he laughs. "When you had offered to sponsor a car wash at my shop and had gotten all wet and I could see through your white t-shirt and saw your perky little nipples saluting me."

A surprised chuckle leaves my lips. "Oh my god," my cheek burned as I swat his chest. "I wasn't that wet. And my nipples weren't hard."

"Uh yeah, I could cut diamonds with them, babe. I think I had to jerk off about three times that night picturing you all lathered up and wet waiting for me just like how you were as you washed my car." He groans as he cups his very noticeably erect penis. My eyes automatically drifted there and turns me on even more.

Noticing where my attention has drifted to, he trails a finger down my neck all the down my spine and towards my stomach. The touch sends sparks through my nervous system. Feeling his touch has always had that effect on me. He finally stops at the button on my shorts and pulls on it once before it pops open.

His blue eyes turn cerulean blue, coated in lust and desire, and love—always love.

Connecting my eyes to his grounds me, giving me a sense of calm that I was seeking earlier when I left and walked off alone. I place my palm on his chest, not to push him away but to feel his heart beating in his chest. It's a soft rumpa pum pum, matching the steady cadence in mine.

"I knew then that if I was beating my dick at the thought of sinking into you it was more than I was ready to admit. I was unequally attracted to you in every way imaginable."

His lips dip down to mine, and I open my mouth,

allowing his tongue entrance to dance with mine. A moan slips out as I lay back in the soft underbrush of the grass and open my legs for him to place himself there.

"I think it's safe to say that we were both attracted to each other beyond a reasonable doubt."

One of his hands slides the zipper down to pull my shorts off and the other reaches underneath my shirt to play with my nipples through my bra. I let out another loud moan, my legs part further, this time canting my hips.

He smirks. "Patience, baby."

He kisses me again as he dips his hand into my black lacy thong as soon as my shorts are off. I feel him slide a finger along my heat, gathering evidence of my arousal before pulling his hand away and offering me up his finger. "Suck," His eyes are nearly pitch black.

I open my mouth at the command. His finger slips into my mouth and I suck my arousal off his finger swirling my tongue around it. I can tell that turns him on because his dick juts out at me, and his hips softly grinds into my pussy.

Fuck.

I wish clothes weren't in the way. My hands seek purchase at the closest thing, which happened to be his shirt and I immediately tug it to get it over his head. In the sexiest move known to mankind, he tugs it off in one swoop, and tosses it over his shoulder. My eyes rake over the rock-hard abs. I never knew a thirty-nine-year-old man can be so devastatingly sexy. If I was standing the man could bring me to my knees.

Not wasting any time, my hands cover every smooth surface as they explore his chest like new territory. But it's not before long where my shirt is the next to go, leaving me in my bra and panties.

"God, you're so beautiful," he says reverently.

I can feel every inch of where his hands land on me.

Laying underneath this man, who holds my heart in his hands, I have never felt so beautiful before. I pull him down to my neck and he uses it as an opportunity to suck down hard on my neck and bite. No doubt left his mark.

He has left me a couple of hickies before in the past, but none where they were visible to anyone else. He is always careful of what he was doing to keep us a secret. I feel this is his way of showing me this is our last night hiding from the world. Claiming me.

"Please," I whisper. My legs circle his hips as I hump him from where I lay. I'm not able to get much friction and I groan in frustration. "Please."

"Please what? Use your words, baby."

This man is so maddening.

"You know what" I can't my hips again, desperate for any type of friction no matter how small.

"Words," his voice is gentle but teasing. "Tell me what you need."

"I need you," I say. His brows raise, indicating he wants me to say more. "I want your mouth. Your hands anything." I'm basically begging at this point. I don't know why he won't put me out of my misery.

"Where?" He places his hands over my hot center and presses down. But not enough where it gives me what I want, only enough to get my attention. "Here?" he asks.

"Yes, please."

"Or my mouth here," Right after he says that, his mouth lands on my nipples as he pulls my bra up to give him access and swirls his tongue around before letting it go with a pop.

"More of that too," I pant. I feel my wetness slide along my leg through my underwear.

"Don't worry." His chuckle is devilish and goose bumps skate along my skin. "I know how to take care of my girl."

There under the cover of the night and with only the

Although We Shouldn't

protection of nature, we made love all night celebrating our union. I felt him fill me up and leave me spent. I remember my last thoughts before falling asleep there in his arms that I had never felt so happy.

But you know what they say about speaking too soon.

10

JAMES

Feather soft fingertips glided over my chest as the sounds of nature greeted me from my slumber. Aside from the random pieces of dirt and twigs sticking me in my back, this was like all the other days where Willow and I were able to spend the night together. She's usually the first person up and would stare at me for hours before I arose, trailing her fingers over me.

I once asked her what she was doing, and she said tracing over the surface of our love. My heart had warmed over while I could barely contain my smile. Kind of like how I am now. Because I took it as a badge of honor to hold all the memories of our love together. It was nothing compared to what she does for me. She held all my darkest days to give me a sliver of sunshine. My forever girl. She giggles, brushing her lips over mine. "Hi." Her voice timid, yet excited. I opened my eyes and pecked her on the lips. By the time we were finished last night, we both agreed we didn't want to go back to the cabin just yet, so we stayed out talking all hours of the night. Sometime between soft whispers and contented sighs we must've fallen asleep. It would've been a great way to wake up on vacation but then reality kicked in.

Today was the day we would tell everyone.

On instinct my muscles locked up. The tension coiling tight and fisting in my gut. Willow sat up feeling the change in me, like I too had reminded her of the struggles that lay ahead of us. I roughed my hand over my face to wake myself up and groaned. As much as I would love for things to be all sunshine, rainbows and open arms, It was naïve to think that everyone would be on board automatically. Especially when you think about all the factors in the equation.

Willow bit her bottom lip as he peered over at me, the worry evident on her face. I sat up and pulled her close to me. Whatever lie ahead of us, she would never have to go through it alone. I told her as much when she wrapped her arms around me. I loved this girl from the bottom of my heart, and I'd die before letting anything break her beautiful fragile heart. I know she was concerned about how her friendship with Serena would weather the storm and I wish I had control over it. I could practically hear all the questions stewing in her mind.

"Tell me what you're thinking," I coaxed gently. Her shoulder lifted impassively as she mumbled into my chest. My fingers floated over her back, rubbing soft reassuring circles. "Remember, I'm worried too. You don't have to be afraid to tell me."

Her eyes lifted up to meet mines. "What if it all goes south. What if they absolutely hate the idea and made you choose."

The question was one that had come across my mind one too many times too. Truth be told, I wouldn't know what to do either. All I knew was that we could only take it one day at a time. They'll be shocked at first sure. But over time maybe they'd start to warm up after it. I refused to believe I'd

Although We Shouldn't

lose my family over this. Because the idea was something I wasn't too keen on allowing to happen. "We can't really tell what would happen. It's a lot to process. Look how long it took for me to admit my feelings for you. And we were in the thick of things. It's going to feel like we're springing it on them out of the blue. They won't understand it at first. But if we ease them into it and just tell them we're dating without the engagement, then over the next couple of weeks we can allow them to adjust."

Her fingers played with the engagement ring on the chain she had it on underneath my shirt she had slept in. We both agreed it would be safer if we waited until after we broke the news to them for her to start wearing it around them. She had wanted to keep it on her at all times, so I gave her the chain to my dog tag for her to string the ring on. I reached a hand out to hold her hand, needing the reassurance she was there with me. My heart thrummed in my chest, frantic, wild and just a tad bit fearful.

"You're right," she gave me a soft smile. "Maybe we should tell them before breakfast though. That way if it's too much no one has anything to throw up." She chuckled nervously over her own joke. Her nose crinkling in worry. I couldn't find it in me to laugh with her. My own stomach was doing somersaults.

"Before breakfast," I agree with her. I looked down at our state of undress and lift my brows. "Let's get dressed and head back over before they get too suspicious and find us missing."

She nods her head in agreement, and we both dress silently, giving each other peaks over shy smiles and soft laughter. It was silly, like we were teenagers having our first morning after encounter. I held onto the idea that the awkwardness and secrecy would soon be over. If I can get through that hurdle, then the worst would be behind us. She hands me my shirt as she slips her own over her head and gathers her intimates in her hands. She stepped forward to start the journey back, but I pull her hand towards me, stopping her from moving any further.

I couldn't let her leave like this. Worried and scared she'd lose it all like she gambled her life away. Not without knowing the cold hard facts. Fact. I love her so much I'd risk the possibility of disrupting my family. Fact. I couldn't live without waking up to her fingertips on my skin. Fact. I was just as scared as her. Fact. I needed just one more kiss like it was my lifeline.

She looks at me questioningly, almost asking *what happened.* Without waiting another minute, I took what I wanted. I grab her head in my hands and meet her lips in a bruising kiss, my tongue coaxing her to allow me entry. She moans, pressing closer to me and granting me access. I let a hand slip to her waist as I softly squeeze it. Once we break apart, she has a soft smile on her face and a blush to her cheeks.

Better. I want that to be the only thing on her mind instead of worrying herself to death. "I love you, babe. Always," I say.

"And Forever," she finishes our mantra.

The rest of the walk to the clearance is in companionable silence. Both of us lost in our thoughts. In hindsight, that was our fault for not paying attention to our surroundings, because we were cut off by Greyson. Fuck. I feel Willow halt behind me, since our hands are connected. She notices him too late to hide her underwear behind her back. But even if she had hid it behind her back, it would still look suspicious. Her hair is wild and unbrushed like someone had ran their hands through her hair. And I hadn't thought to button up my jeans, thinking I had time before anyone was up to sneak in and take a quick shower. I got lazy. Another mistake.

Although We Shouldn't

Willow was still sporting a mean blush for our kiss. The evidence alone was staggering.

I watch as a myriad of emotions flit across his face before he settled on one. Anger.

"What the fuck is going on?" He looks between us, daring us to lie to him.

I squeeze Willows hand in support. Her eyes are wide and alarmed as she looks at me on how to handle this. I wish I knew. I hadn't been prepared for this scenario. I hadn't banked on being caught. Nerves gather, catching in my throat making it hard for me to swallow.

"Is anyone going to answer me?" He asks baffled. "Because trust me, you wouldn't believe the thoughts going through my head right now, and I would love for either of you to put them to rest."

I can feel Willow shaking next to me. I need to step up. Take control of this situation. I hold my free hand out in a bid to calm him down. To make him see reason. "It's not as bad as it looks." Hopefully. "Maybe we can wait until everyone has breakfast to have this conversation." I grappled for any type of strength as I watch his face scrunch up in annoyance. My heart pounded like an 808 drum, as I waited for him to talk. The longer I had to wait, the more I wanted to fill the silence with more words. Like it'll somehow magically make everything right if I found the right words.

"Maybe you should close your jeans before you talk to anyone else, yeah?" His brow lifts on his forehead, but his face was impassively void of any emotion. Greyson was always great at bottling his emotions up. As a kid, we always tried to push him to be more expressive. Weather it was a smile or a laugh or even some anger. Now, I was scared for the mask to slip off him. He was always the wild card.

I zip my pants up, briefly letting go of Willow's hand. "Please. Can't we just wait for some coffee is at least in our system?" To buy us more time. I need more time to think about how to tell him. To tell everyone. This wasn't the way I had saw everything going down in my head. I wanted to break it to them gently, ease them into the idea of us. Especially since Greyson had expressed his feelings to Willow last night. I'm worried about his mental state. This can't be easy for him to take in. Not so soon on the cusp of heartbreak.

He brushes my comment off, ignoring me and focuses on Willow. "He's the guy you're seeing, isn't he? Or are you fucking other people too?" He tosses the disrespectful comment casually, which makes her flinch.

"It's him." her voice is a lot stronger than I thought it would have come out and there's a defiant lift of her chin. She's always been headstrong and confident. I see some of her strength returning in her blue eyes. My heart fills with pride as she stands up for herself. As much as I would love to do most of the talking to carry the weight of the backlash, I know she had to defend herself when the time comes for it.

"He's twice your age, Willow. What can you possibly expect him to give you? Kids?" His face turns a little green at the thought.

"What's wrong with having kids with him?" Her arms cross over her chest. "I'm sure his sperm works fine." I never given much consideration to having more kids, but the thought of having one with her, seeing her round with my kid in her belly is a dream I'd like to make a reality.

"That's fucking sick, Willow. He's my dad, and you're—you're," he stammers over his words getting angrier by the moment.

"I'm what?" She prods him.

I walk over to her and pull her to me. Now that the cat's out of the bag, I won't be apart from her another moment while we face our first hurdle as a couple. My hand moves to her lower back to give her silent support.

Although We Shouldn't

"Sick, that's what it is. You're just a mid-life crisis. There's no real future with him." Hearing these words from my son is a huge blow. I knew he'd have a hard time accepting it, but hearing how badly he thinks of me hurts.

"She's more than that—" I start to explain but am cut off by the harsh glare of his eyes. Eyes he got from me.

He lets out a harsh disbelieving chuckle. "And why should I listen to a word you say? Look what you're doing. You're no damn role model." his voice is harsh and sharp, cutting me down to the quick. "I'll never accept this. You and her." His mouth curls in distaste. "She's not permanent and you know it."

He's my son. I keep reminding myself. I don't want to see him hurt. But I refuse to stand here and listen to him say one more thing that disrespects my girl and our relationship. "Careful," I warn him. Hurt people hurt people, I remind myself. It doesn't make it right, though.

"No, you be careful. Before Mom comes out and find you out with the trash."

In one quick movement, I have him up against the tree with my hands holding him hostage. It's not enough force to hurt him, but enough to grab his attention. "Don't you say another fucking word about the love of my life, or I swear to god," I growl.

His face grows white, and tears brim his eyes. In that second, he's my five-year-old little man. The guy who would follow me around at work and ask me questions about my job. He'd help me fix his mom's car. He's the ten-year-old who danced with his little sister at her grade school dance because she couldn't make any friends yet. He was my little boy, who was hurting, because of me.

I sighed dropping my head to his—father to son. "I'm sorry you had to find out this way. But please don't ask me to give her up. Because I can't. I won't." My voice is hoarse, coated in pain and desperation. How do I undo all this damage? What can I do at this point?

"What about mom?" He asks, voice cracking. "She won't be okay with this? How would she feel knowing you're dating someone her daughter's age?"

Looking him straight in the eye, I say, "I don't know. But I'm not breaking up with Willow. I can't." I hope he can hear my love for her fill my voice. Hear how much this is tearing me up on the inside.

"What about me?" The first tear slips from his eye. How I wish I can make this all go away from him. A way to erase the pain. "I love her, dad."

"I love her too." It's the only thing I can say to him. I see the moment he accepts this is all he ever gets out of me. His body deflates and the fight leaves him. He glances her way and I want to stand in front of her, shield her from the judgment he has in his eyes. All he does though, is look sad and defeated.

"I could have given you everything," he says to her.

"He is everything," she moves to me and wraps an arm around my waist. My chest fills with pride as I hear her make her claim on me. This was our first hurdle and we managed it well.

I spoke too soon because the next words out of his mouth is, "Don't expect any fucking welcome from me. Good luck telling my mother and Serena. You know, your best friend. His daughter. I'm sure they'll welcome you with open arms."

I feel her go ramrod straight next to me before she clears her throat. "However they react, I'm sure it'll be fine."

"James? Greyson?" I hear Elaine call out, followed by the slight crunch of her footsteps as she walks our way.

He laughed, dark and hollow. "Looks like you're about to find out."

Fuuuck. I send a silent prayer up to the big man upstairs

and ask him to do me a solid and make this encounter easier than the last. Willow has my hand in a death grip. Her face turns pale. She rounds her shoulders like she's preparing for battle. It may not be the best time, but I bend down and press a kiss to her forehead and tilt her eyes up to me. "It'll be okay. You and me, right?"

I'm sending her all the encouragement I have while simultaneously trying to draw my own strength. She opens her mouth to answer but is cut off by a screech.

"What the fuck is going on?" Elaine's hand is at her throat like she couldn't possibly handle the sight before her. Behind her, Serena isn't too far behind. Great, the gangs are all here. "Well, is anyone going to answer me?"

My son just glares at where my hand is located on her face in silence. His way of letting us know we're on our own. When Serena finally makes her way to us, she eyes us curiously. "What's going on, Mom? I could hear you a mile away. What's with the level 200 freak out?"

I close my eyes and ready to brace myself. I pull Willow closer to me and hold her hand. A show of solidarity. Facing everything head-on, I look each of them in the eyes, so they know I'm serious. "Willow and I are together."

Shock is in everyone's face, everyone except Greyson, thanks to him getting the show of a lifetime.

"What the fuck do you mean together?" Elaine whispers hoarsely. As if one of her high society friends will find out if she speaks any higher. Her fingers tremble and her lips tighten in a thin line. Her dark black hair is tied up around her face and she reaches up to smooth it down in a nervous bid for some control.

"We're getting married," Willow says next to me. Her eyes reach mine. I'm with you, she silently says.

I waited for it. For everyone to blow up like Greyson had. *In three, two, one...*

Serena tosses her head back and laughs. "Oh my god. Good one. You had me fooled. Seriously, guys, what the fuck is going on?"

That's when Willow reaches behind her in her back pocket and places her engagement ring on her finger. It takes two seconds for everyone to register the new addition.

"This is some fucking joke." Elaine bellows out. She looks ready to explode.

I move Willow behind me protectively. I know how Elaine can get when she's mad and never want Willow to be subjected to it. "I know this is hard for you to process. But I want you to know that this is it for me. It's her who I love."

"Love?" Serena asks incredulously. "Dad come on. She's my age. That's sick."

There's that word again. They throw it around like our love is wrong when it's nothing but pure. I ask the man upstairs for guidance, a way to get me through this. I doubt he'll answer this prayer, since my last one went unanswered.

"And what, she's going to be my stepmom? Do you see how wrong that is on so many levels? She's my roommate, dad." Serena throws out. Fresh tears streamed down her face. This is going wrong. So, so wrong.

"Roommate?" Willow asks softly. Her face is crestfallen. Hurt washes over her face.

"You can't seriously believe we're still friends after this." A disbelieving laugh echoes around us as Serena shakes her head.

"You said a few days ago that you'd be happy for me. That even if he was older than me, as long as I was happy, it'd be okay." Willow's voice shakes.

I squeeze her midsection, wishing I could have a moment alone with her to talk to her. Give her the reassurance she needs. As it stands, the worst has yet to come. I'm proven right as Elaine walks over to us.

Although We Shouldn't

"You should probably leave." She stares Willow down, not letting up. "No, you should definitely leave."

"She's not going anywhere," I growl. I'll leave with her if that's the case. It's time they accept we're a package deal. Where she goes, I go. "She's been a part of this family for years now. Nothing changes."

Elaine whips her glare to me. "Family? That's rich coming from you. Where was this mentality when you were busy fucking a child."

Willow flinches again.

"She's twenty-five. Not a fucking child."

"She's the same age as Serena James. Or did you happen to forget that as you got your dick wet?" She wets her lips as her chest heaves up and down. "Look at her, James. What were you hoping to gain from this? To tear your family further apart? How did you think Serena would feel knowing you were going behind our backs and getting your rocks off with her best friend."

"Say one more word about her, I dare you." I step toe to toe with her. I'd never put my hands on a woman; however, she's making it hard for me to refrain myself.

"What about us, James? I thought this was our second chance."

"It was never going to be you," I say softly. No matter how angry at her I am right now, I would never intentionally hurt her feelings. "You are the mother of our two beautiful children. And I love you. But not in that way. Not ever again."

"I thought…" she whispers. Her eyes cast a sheen.

This is hard for everyone and I'm hoping on a tight thread that this doesn't cause irreparable damage to my family and my relationship with them. The air is thick with tension as everyone is silent, processing the events of this morning. How is it a day can turn so rotten so fast with one decision? One moment in time. We are afforded a thousand moments that make up the fabric of our lives. One decision shouldn't have the impact of a TNT bomb, destroying everything in its wake.

"We never meant to hurt anyone," Willow offers. "We just found our way to each other." There my girl goes being strong and facing things head-on, no apologies in sight. And damn right. We have nothing to apologize for. When two people fall in love, they don't look to hurt anyone in the process. There's no stopping the magnitude of their love either. They are forever bound to one another, their destinies bound and tethered.

At the sound of Willow's voice, Elaine snaps out of it and casts her another glare. "Why are you still here?" her voice could wither the strongest man. Not Willow though. "You are no longer welcome. Go home."

"Ms. Hannigan, please just let me explain." Willow reaches her hand out. An olive branch and I almost want to pull her back. Tell her there's nothing for her to explain. I realize, though, this is something she needs to do, a silent girl code.

Only, Elaine leaves her hanging and steps back. "There is nothing for you here."

Willow looks around us for help. Greyson looks down, cutting off eye contact. When her eyes land on Serena's, Serena's eyes tear up before she, too, looks away. Next, they land on mine, and mine scream the loudest—only in support. Telling her I'm here. I'm not going anywhere. Her lips tremble and her breath hitches.

"Stay," I whisper to her, turning my back on my family. I need a moment with her. Fuck it, two moments. They can stew in their misery alone for a few seconds. "Hey, look at me. I'm right here."

"How are we going to get through this?" Her voice shakes, caught in her inner turmoil. I wish I had a definitive answer

Although We Shouldn't

for her. To tell her it'll blow over, like I used to assure her. Now that we're in the thick of things, I can't make those assurances. All I can offer her is my undying love and pray that it's enough for her.

I'm disappointed in Serena for turning her back on her best friend.

Especially in a time when she could use it the most.

"Stay with me, okay? You're not alone." A vow. One I would never break.

We turn back to face everyone and still, no one has yet to make eye contact with her. I love my family with all my heart, but it hurts my soul to see them treat her this way. When they used to always greet her with a warm smile and open arms. She's the same girl they always knew. If they can't accept us under these new conditions, it'll be a tough road for everyone.

Making up my mind, I pull her with me as we begin to walk together back to the cabin.

"Where are you going, James?" Elaine asks at my back.

"If she's not welcome here, then I'm leaving with her."

"If you go, don't come back," that came from Serena.

My heart cracks in half. I couldn't imagine not being in my little girl's life. She just got engaged. I always imagined I'd get to walk her down the aisle. My shoulders stand tall and my jaw clenches in frustration that this is where it's leading to. What else can I say to them to make them see it doesn't have to be either or?

I would never make them choose between me and anyone else. I expected tough conversations. Not an impasse at all sides. I guess Willow and I both hoped for too much too soon. I can only hope that over time, they'll begin to accept us. Willow's hand slid from mine and my head turned to her questioningly.

My heart knew what my brain was trying to catch up on.

Her eyes begged me to forgive her, but I didn't know what she wanted was forgiveness for before it was too late. Anxious energy whipped between her as she walked a few steps away from me. I felt the distance already piling between us.

"I'm so sorry," her voice cracked at the last word. "I can't do this." With no further explanation, she fled the scene, taking my heart with her. She barely left me time to call after her.

Serena grabbed my hand, stopping me from walking after her. "Let her go, dad." My heart clamored in my chest, rebelling against the fissure Willow put in my heart.

"How can you say that?" I asked her. How can they have said any of the things that transpired?

"Trust me, it's for the best." Her voice was apologetic, yet her eyes were unrelenting.

She was wrong though.

Being away from your heart was never the right thing to do.

But what can you do when they're in two different locations?

11

WILLOW

Tears are useless. I always hated the concept of crying. I despised it even more when my body shook viciously as I held in my tears. It was like my entire being wanted to rebel against my wishes. Even now, as my mascara streamed down my face and my tears tracked down my cheeks, I couldn't find solace in it. They—my tears—got in the way of everything. They blurred my vision as I hastily packed everything in my favorite red suitcase. I could only see a vague outline of my belongings, but my shaky hands reached out and grabbed them only to stuff them haphazardly in the open luggage.

You should probably leave.

The words stung, even as I repeated the words Elaine said to me. A woman who had always been another mother figure to me. The mother of my best friend. But her eyes didn't hold the usual warmth they usually did when she looked at me with her million-dollar smile. Her mouth was screwed like she tasted something foul in her mouth, and I was the cause. The acid that was threatening to ruin everything she stood for, to destroy her peace. Her eyes didn't hold any anger then either, looking back on it.

No, it held frustration and sadness. And above all else, there was pain.

Because of me.

My breath stuttered as my nervous system tried to regulate itself. I was so stupid to think they would accept our love. It was unorthodox. Foreign. Taboo. Every one of their eyes held a level of distrust. I could only guess the reasons why. Hiding it from them for one thing. Betrayal for another. Elaine welcomed me into her home, and I stole the only man she's ever loved, whether it was intentional or not didn't matter to her. Serena, my best friend, the one I thought I could rely on no matter what the situation was, had looked at me with pity in her eyes. She had been hoping her parents would get back together. She didn't care much for our love story. It was written in the way she closed herself off to me. The more her mother cried, the further she stepped away from me. I couldn't hold eye contact with anyone in her family. The air had become stifling, even though we were outside. So, I'd been cast out of their group, where I was once always welcomed, and forced to weather this turbulent storm by myself. And Jay. *My* Jay. He was torn, he wanted to pick up the pieces of his family, at least with his kids, and help them through this, but he also wanted to go with me. to assure me, to comfort me. I saw the indecision in his eyes. His eyes flitted around, landing on each of us, trying to figure out who to tend to first. He wanted to fix this. He had hope. And hope was a dangerous thing to have. There were no guarantees in hope. His hands held onto mine, almost like if he held on tight enough, he could preserve us, keep me tethered to him just a little bit more.

But I could see what he couldn't. Serena loved her parents, she wanted them back together, and Greyson

Although We Shouldn't

couldn't wrap his head around this new information. He didn't understand it—the age gap or how we could possibly love each other. Or rather *how* we thought we could. His head kept shaking like he was ruling out the thoughts in his head. Conflicted with his own turbulent feelings.

I was the threat now. And they banded together to unify around their mom. I couldn't fault them for that.

But I hadn't expected them to dispel me out of their fold so quickly.

You should probably leave.
You should probably leave.
You should probably leave.

It was running on a continuous loop in my head. I imagine this is what Satan felt like being cast out of heaven. The fallen angel disbound and shunned from all that he knew. I sniffled and wiped the new tears that have fallen onto my face. My chest feels like a ten-pound overhaul truck is sitting on top of my chest, and my lungs are working overtime just to breathe. I drop to my knees, pushing my hand under the bed to see if any stray items may have rolled underneath there. My hand catches on a lone bra. I pause.

This was the bra I wore on our very first night here. James and I were the first ones to arrive. We had planned it that way. Selfishly, we wanted time to ourselves before we would tell everyone the news. He couldn't keep his hands off me. We were caught up in euphoria and I secretly loved the feeling of freedom. It felt like I was finally getting everything I wanted. Looking back, we were quite reckless when we got lost in each other. We nearly got caught the first time, had it not been for Greyson coming in and slamming the door behind him. Funny how things work out in the end. I slid out from underneath the bed on my knees and held the bra in my hands, looking at it. A sigh escapes me, providing little to no relief. And why should I have relief? It feels the there's a permanent red letter on my chest. Forever imprisoning me to my sins. The weight of my actions—our actions—nearly crushed me. What I would give for a second chance to do things right. But one thing for certain, I wouldn't take back my relationship with James. I could never. I'd find a way to tell them first. Maybe it wouldn't be such a huge blow to them. Maybe I'd tell Serena first. If only to have someone who's in my corner. I had to have hoped she would be happy for me. How could she not? I'm her best friend.

Or was her best friend.

Our friendship is hanging on a tightrope, I presume. I couldn't just call her up and ask her to meet me at our spot underneath the willow tree. What would she say to me that could make me feel better? What would I say? The look in her eye was staggering. She looked at me as if she hardly recognized me, and that hurt. She knew me inside and out. She knew all my secrets, aside from the elephant in the room. She's the only person I trust with the other hard-kept secret of my bad perm circa 2005. But you would hardly believe it as her eyes slid off me and aimed at the floor. Like I was no one. A stranger. No one.

"Willaford." The familiar smell of pinecones and grease greets my nose, making me cry even harder. The room was silent save for the sound of his heavy footsteps and a couple of rough exhales from me as I contained my cries. I perfected the art of silence. Holding in the strongest emotions so no one would find out what was going on. Silent moans? Check. Silent scoff? Check. Silent laughter? Checkity check. I was a master of holding it in, which comes in quite handy right about now. If he knew how much pain I was in, he would pick me hands down. And I refused to let him choose me over his family. Holding in the anguish of my cries was a small price to pay for what I had to do next.

His gravelly voice put shards of glass through my heart,

Although We Shouldn't

which only rips me apart even more. I can hear the plea his tone carried. To understand, to help make things better, to come to him. He used my full name, though. That alone told me things were bad if I hadn't already known. "Baby girl, look at me." He pleads.

"No," it was a whisper. A desperate plea for him to not make it harder for me. A demand to not lie and say we can work through it. It was all I could muster at this point. I didn't trust my voice not to break down in front of him. He had enough on his plate with his family. I could only imagine the carnage I left in my wake. The least I could do was hold it together for him. Later, when I'm home by myself and I can have the space to break down and spiral as much as I'd like, that's when I'll allow myself to fall apart.

Not now.

"Please," I feel his heat at my back as he drops onto his knees. I clench my eyes closed tightly, trembling at his nearness. I want to fall apart in his hands and allow him to kiss the hurt away. My fists clench tightly, and the imprint of my engagement ring slices through my hand. I wish we had more time. That would be the only way to fix this. But only for a little while. A day ago, this would have been heaven. I always loved feeling his heat envelop me. But now? Now it was hell, in the most excruciating way, because I knew it would be the last time that I get to feel the luxury of being comforted by the man who made being in love so fucking easy.

"This will blow over, just watch, baby." His voice cracked on the last word, and his head leaned against the back of mine. Even he didn't believe his own words. He wanted to, though. And maybe if all it took was believing something would happen, could happen, then maybe this would play out a lot differently.

But that was for fairy tales and wishful thinking.

This was reality.

The bitch. She never liked me.

My heart pulled and thrashed around in my chest, begging for mercy. My heart begged me not to make any hasty decisions I would regret later. It would be too easy to just give in and pretend what he said was true. But I knew that if it came down to it, and he had to choose, I would never forgive myself for letting him make either decision. Serena's distrustful eyes flashed in my mind and Elena's cries rang in my head.

You?!

You?!

You?!

"And what if...What if it doesn't?" I voice the real question he's too afraid to answer, breaking through the echoes of my subconscious. "Would you be able to choose between me and your family if it came down to it?"

I feel his wince. Sharp and quick like a whip. He knew as much as I did—and still do—that although the choice would be hard, it would still break my heart.

No. I'm sparing him the pain and suffering from making the impossible decision. His arms wound around my torso and squeezed me like sheer force alone could keep me with him. *Oh, love. If only that were possible.* My lower trip trembles and I hold in another cry that wants to break loose. My eyes squeeze to hold the damn that wants to break loose. Lifting myself up, I feel his hold tighten even more, constricting me and causing my emotions to be. But still, I continue packing, searching for the last of my items, and zipping up my travel bag. If I stop now, I may never leave. And that was never an option.

You should leave.

You should leave.

The words in my head were like an alarm ringing out into

Although We Shouldn't

the distance, alerting passersby that danger was coming—me. I was the danger. It was still hard to wrap my head around that. Although, I suppose we were all a threat to each other now. The fabric of the lives we hold onto by a thread can snap by a single decision. It's like a game of emotional warfare and the winner is chosen by a game of rock, paper, scissors.

Before I can lift it up, though, his hand lands on mine. His other hand lifts my chin and connects our eyes. Blue. The color I come to love and associate with the best man I know. *Please don't.* I already feel my resolve crumbling, and any minute I'll break down and ruin all my hard work of keeping my composure together. Whatever he's about to say will break me.

I'm sure of it.

His eyes are turbulent and passionate, sucking me into the depth of his unyielding soul. I see all the promises he made and all the ones he has to break. Like my heart. I see everything in his eyes. He was never able to hide his truths from me. It was how I knew he loved me as more than his daughter's best friend before the words were ever spoken.

"Just wait, Willow. Don't go. She's hurt, but she'd never kick you out." His other hand came to grab my face. "I know my ex-wife. I know her. She's a compassionate woman. She loves you like her own daughter. She didn't mean it." His eyes track every movement I make and pull me tighter to him. Begging the universe to not be so cruel to us.

"She does." I'm as sure of it as I was sure of my own feelings for him. Elena without a doubt wanted me gone, and I couldn't fault her for that. Could I? The blame landed solely on my shoulders. Always, always, my fault.

"How can you be so sure?"

"Because if I knew I lost you to someone else, I wouldn't want to see her every day." I'd want her dead. I wouldn't want any reminders of him with another woman. I wouldn't want to hear her voice, see her face, or make nice. Love is messy when more than two people are involved. I was the former student turned teacher in this department. I could write an entire thesis on it. Because when have I ever been able to just be in love and have someone love me back without any complications? But fuck, wouldn't it have been nice? More tears track down my lids as I tremble in his arms. My hands land on his and pry his fingers off my face.

"Tell me what to do," the tremor in his voice cracks my already fractured heart even more. His eyes beg me to stay. But we both know that I can't. "This can't be it. There is no me without you, Willow. I am the Earth revolving around you. You showed me the beauty of love again. And you're telling me it's going to be ripped away from me?" Pain oozes from his words and tears leak from his eyes.

If anyone doubted if there was any beauty to pain, all they'd have to do would be to look at him now. With sorrow in his eyes and his face contorted from the pain I was undoubtedly causing him, he's still the most beautiful man I've ever met. "Always and forever, remember?" he begs. "Say it."

"I can't." I cry at the reminder of what almost was.

"Say it." He stands and towers over me but remains nonthreatening. With him, I am always safe. "Always," he whispers and picks up my hand once again, eyes locked on the engagement ring. He repeats the phrase over and over, hoping I'll finish it. But it takes me back to when we first made the promise.

I was a different girl back then.

. . .

Although We Shouldn't

1 *Year Ago*
The music playing on high-definition speakers washed out the screaming thoughts building in my head. I don't know how I found myself here. Although wherever here is I wasn't sure of. It was an old bar in the middle of some unknown town. Over time, as James and I had begun to hide away in secret places, finding hidden places became my solace. Away from familiar stares, I could think and breathe fresh air. Back home, the air was stale and thick with distrust. I hated secrecy. At first, it was fun.

Now, it wasn't.

He told me it was nothing and that I should trust him. James had been set up on a blind date by Manny. He said that he needed to get out more. All night I sat up in bed wondering about his night. Was she pretty? Did she make him laugh like I do? Does she want to get married? Was he going to take her home?

The last thought soured my gut and had me out the door in less than five minutes. I needed an escape. So here I was. People of all walks of life filtered the small space as I weaved my way through the closed space. Some small band was playing a hauntingly beautiful song that perfectly matched how I felt.

Beer.

I needed alcohol if I was going to get through the night.

My eyes scanned the area as I found my way to the bar. "One beer on tap please." I'm normally a margarita girl, but something about the eye piercing and rugged tattoos told me I wouldn't find that here. Whatever. Anything would work fine with me. When he placed the glass in front of me with a napkin, I gulped it down in one sitting.

The bartender raised a brow in question but said nothing as he stared at me.

"Another one please." I placed some cash on the table.

The smell of pinecones and aftershave filled my senses as a rough voice pushed my money away. "She's cut off for the night."

I wilted and turned to the intruder. "What are you doing here? Aren't you supposed to be on your date?"

"It ended early." James stocky build covered my vision and my body naturally wilted toward him. I loved this man so much. Couldn't he see that? Why did he need to go on a blind date? Or any date for that matter when he had me? I was being unfair to him. I know that. I couldn't help the jealousy festering in my veins making me feel like a ticking bomb.

"Oh." It was all I could say. My stupid little hard did a happy dance in my chest. All the questions I wanted to know bubbled u inside me. Why did it end early? What happened? What does it mean?

I watched James pay for my drink out of the corner of my eye. My body swayed to the next song the band was playing, something about lost hearts and promises of forever. Once he was done, James reached for my hand and led us away from the bar and toward the door.

Whether it was the one beer in me or the fact we were far away from everyone we knew, something in me didn't want to leave just yet.

"One dance," I asked him.

He nodded his head and led me to the dancefloor where I laid my head on his chest, and he wrapped his arms around me. My entire body screamed "meant to be."

"What am I going to do with you?" It was a gentle tease, but I answered the question with an honest answer.

"Never let me go."

I felt his arms tighten around me, and it became my favorite thing he did. He looked handsome in his dark-washed jeans and white button-down shirt. I inhaled his scent letting it fill me up and overtake my senses. I felt the deep rumble of his chuckle through his chest and smiled.

"It was never a question."

My head lifted as I stared into his eyes demanding an answer. "Then why'd you go on the date at all?" Why? When he had me?

"What was I going to say? No? They'd ask why I couldn't go or didn't want to go. What acceptable answer would I have to go give them?" He made a lot of sense, too bad my heart was being unreasonable. I hated feeling this way. Out of control and desperate. He's never made me feel that way until now. Until the possibility of losing him was real.

"You want to know something else?" he asked after a few moments of silence.

"What?" I asked sourly. If he came here to tell me the date was great, I was going to sock him in the nuts. Because I didn't need to hear that shit.

"I learned I don't need to date anyone else. I was on a date with a perfectly beautiful woman— ouch!" he rubbed his arm from where I had punched him. Served him right for saying that to me. He grabbed me by the arms and met my eyes. "But," he emphasized. "I will always love you," he said.

My heart kick-started. A desperate fool to hear him say it again. The corner of my lips lifted in a shy smile. "You love me?" It was the first time he had said it to me. Not the most promising time to confess your love to someone. Right after he left a date. "But he left the date for you," my heart screams at me.

"Always," he smirks before taking me in a searing kiss that I could feel all the way to my toes.

"And forever," I promised him.

"And forever..." I whisper back brokenly. Those words are the ones to break the dam. Rivers stream down my face and I fall into his arms. How did we get here? How do we get back to where we were.

"You promised, Willow," His tears soak my neck as we hold onto each other.

I'm running out of time. I already feel my resolve slipping. My body softens and molds to him. I don't know where to go from here other than to leave, no matter how much I wish I could stay or take him with me.

This is where our road ends. So, I muster up some energy and break away from him once again, promising myself this is the last time because I can't stand to do it anymore. "Maybe when the dust is cleared, we can find our way back. But for right now, I need to go, and you need to stay. Figure things out with your family."

His head is already shaking in dismissal. "No, not if it means losing you."

God damn, my heart. I must stay strong. "You're not losing me." At least I hope not.

"Then put the ring back on," His hands move to mine and force it back on me. I try to push it away, but he closes his hand around mine. "If you're still mine, keep it on. Please." He huffs a breath. "It's the only way I can let you walk out of here if it's what you need to do."

He's not being fair. But I don't have any more energy left to fight, so I leave it on my finger—heavy and glaring and painful. "Fine."

I gather my bags and head for the door before giving him one last look.

Who knew love could be so painful?

Later when I'm back in my room I let the tears roam free. I cry hard and fast, asking God why he would give me something so beautiful and pure and mine only to rip it away from me. I cry so hard that I run to the bathroom and purge the contents of my stomach.

This is the way it'll be from now on, I think.

Alone and miserable.

12

JAMES

Four Weeks Later

"Hey it's Willow. If you're the unlucky person receiving this message, then that means your shit out of luck." She chuckles before continuing, "I'm busy at the moment, so leave me a message and tell me what's on your mind and I'll get back to you." The message ends before a beep sounds.

I've reached her voicemail again for the millionth time.

Things between my family have come to a head after the disastrous weekend and everything came out. Elaine is back to bickering with me, picking little fights while my Serena and Greyson...well my kids refuse to talk to me. Only offering short words here and there and doing the mandatory check-ins with me.

"Hey, dad. All is good. No, nothing exciting happened today. Okay talk you later bye."

"Hey, Dad. No, no wedding plans have made yet. I gotta go, bye."

I haven't been to work in the past two weeks, which I know isn't the best way to handle the stress, but it's the best I can do now. I had tried to distract myself from the turmoil of my life by throwing myself into work, which has been proven to be futile since I almost injured myself not paying attention to what I was doing as got burned while fixing the motor of an old motorcycle.

Something had to give and by the looks of it I had to make the first move. Reaching out from my pocket, I grabbed my phone and sent the first text of many.

Me: Where are you?

My fingers drummed on the counter as I awaited a reply from my daughter. I figured I'd start with the easiest hurdle. Of everyone I had to have a conversation with, she was the easiest, only because she had the least emotions invested in what had gone down. She wasn't an unbiased third party, just more manageable to deal with. I wasn't going to get any answers or resolutions by waiting on my ass for them to come to me. I had to go to them, It was a good twenty minutes before I got a response.

Serena: Just pulled up to Mom's why?

Without replying to her, I grabbed my keys and headed out the door. It was less than ideal to talk to her at her mother's, risking the chance she might be there. If I told her my plans, she might dip out before I get there and leave me hanging in the dust. It was better to talk to her face to face.

My hands were warm and clammy as I wiped them down the length of my jeans. There was no easy way to have this conversation, so I braced myself for all types of reactions. Serena's car I had gotten her had been traded up for a newer version, a white, sleep two-door Porsche her fiancee had gotten her was still in the driveway, which was a good sign she was still here.

Although We Shouldn't

Pushing my shoulders back, I tested the doorknob and twisted it before opening it up and stepping inside. It seemed like forever ago when we were all gathered here preparing for a family vacation. The halls had been filled with life and chatter. Everyone was chatting over each other, as they prepared to leave.

My eyes go to the hallway that led to the bathroom I was in with Willow before shaking my head and clearing my throat. "Anybody here?" I called out before I heard the sounds of the television playing in the background. Following where the sound was, my footsteps took me closer to whoever was holding court in the living. I sent a prayer that it was Serena and not Elaine. As I rounded the hall, I peeped along the wall and released a breath. It was Serena.

She was sitting alone with her feet curled up on the sofa and a blanket over her shoulders. "Euphoria" was playing on the television while a bowl of popcorn covered in chocolate syrup sat on the coffee table.

Walking the rest of the distance over to her, I stopped beside her and waited for her to acknowledge me. I stood awkwardly through a scene of bare breasts and heavy sounds on the television before I cleared my throat, hoping to catch her attention. Her gaze remained on the show, though I knew she knew I was right there.

I sighed. I walk over to the TV and shut it off before moving her bowl of popcorn aside to sit across from her. My fingers steepled as I directed my full attention to her. She had her arms crossed and a mean pout on her lips while her eyes avoided mine.

Undeterred by the cold front, I cleared my throat again and began. I decided it was better to be as honest as possible instead of skating around the truth. "Willow and I weren't planned. It wasn't something either of us thought would happen."

She scoffs, rolling her eyes.

My daughter could be stubborn when she wants, this being one of those times.

Nonetheless, I continued, "Truth," I scratched the scuff along my beard. "It started as a friendship. We'd talk to each other. Help each other navigate life. It was purely platonic. Your mother and I had been at each other's throats before the divorce. And Willow," I allowed myself to pause to get the right words out. I needed her to see, none of our actions had any malicious intent behind our actions. "Willow was a good person to talk to. She listens when you need to. Offers sage advice, though for her age I wasn't expecting much, but she is so smart, wise beyond her years. She made me feel like things were less insufferable. She even tried to help me with your mom when things were rough. She'd seen a great deal of your mother and I going at it behind the scenes. The only one who really knew and saw it all."

"If she helped you with Mom, how did it turn to this?" She waved her hand in front of me to clarify what this was. Though, I'm guessing she means our relationship. I'm hoping we still have a relationship, since I haven't heard from her.

I allow a small smile remembering it all. The images play through my mind like a flip book. "It didn't happen overnight, believe it or not." I paused letting the information sink in.

She reclines in her seat and peeks at me. It gives me hope she'll be recessive to what I have to say. She motions her fingers signaling for me to continue.

"We went about our lives like normal. Aside from the occasional conversations we'd have, we barely talked. But in those talks, it developed to a friendship. One where we'd share our likes and dislikes, and bonded over seventies music."

Serena allows a soft chuckle to come out. "God her and

that music. It drove me crazy." She faces me fully and asks a harder question. "So, what changed? If it was just friendship?"

"I did. Or we both did. We started hanging out more. As friends of course. And I felt things in me shift. Subtly. Slowly. We had almost instances, near misses, but nothing had happened yet. I wasn't comfortable with these changes. Because she's your age. She's young enough to be my daughter. But one day, she went out on a date with some guy, Dirk or whoever. I heard you on the phone with her talking through outfit ideas."

Another roll of her eyes. "Kirk. He was such a tool."

The name rings a bell, and I nod my head. "I remember having the strongest urge to tell her not to go. To stay home. Or better yet, hang out with me. But I couldn't do that, could I? I mean, I had no right. She wasn't my daughter. I had no other right to make those demands. And that was when I knew I wanted to. That night changed everything."

"What did you do?" Doubt colors her eyes and her brows lower in confusion. Though we both could probably tell what happened next.

"I found out where she was and made my move. I kissed her," I stated matter-of-factly and watched Serena's face for her reaction.

Her face curls in disgust, though there's no anger there. So, I guess it's safe to assume it's from picturing us kissing and not her initial reaction in thinking we were wrong. "Oh my god. You were her mystery kisser? That's just gross, Dad." She said, though there was humor in her voice.

"It was a slow build for us. We took our time. It was new waters for both of us. And we were very scared you guys would find out and hate us. It was easier for us to hide rather than come out and confess everything. But, when I proposed, we both knew it couldn't be a secret anymore. We wanted to tell you guys, not find out the way you did."

Serena's nose scrunches in distaste. "I do not feel bad for Greyson. He told me what he walked in on, and I have to say, my eyes would need a lot of bleach to erase that image out of my head."

I grimace. "We were reckless. And I do regret he found out that way. We had other ideas in mind. Ideas that involved clothes. Lots of clothes and no body parts exposed. But we don't regret you finding out. At least I don't."

"But what about mom?" She asks cautiously. "She was so hopefully you guys could try again.

"Honey, I love your mom." Serena's eyes light up and I hold a hand up. "But I'm not in love with her. My heart belongs to someone else." I look at her pointedly, so I don't have to outright say it.

She deflates and groans, holding her hands over her eyes. "But my best friend?" She shivers. "Dad, how am I going to look her in the eye knowing she did the dirty tango with my dad." She holds a hand to her stomach.

Scooting over to her side, I wrap my arms around her and pull her to me. "With grace. I know it's going to take some time to get used to. But I'm hoping that you will come to accept it. I would have to feel like I have to choose, though she did it for me. At least for now." My heart pangs in my chest thinking if the last time I spoke to Willow, my ray of sunshine. My days have been cloudy since she left the cabin that weekend. I wanted to give her space and allow her to come back to me on her own.

Serena pulls away. "What do you mean?"

"She left that weekend, and I haven't heard from her since then. She said she didn't want me to choose between you guys and her." Serena's eyes soften in empathy. I'm not trying to make her feel bad, only to be as truthful as I can be. "I

Although We Shouldn't

know you guys had some words that day, or rather you. I hope you guys patch things up since you all live together. Haven't you spoken to her?

She winces. "I kind of sort of haven't been back to our apartment since that weekend. I haven't been the greatest best friend these past few weeks." Her face reddens in embarrassment. "Oh my god and the last thing I said to her was she wasn't my best friend."

"Yeah, that was not cool by the way." My eyes point at her, so she gets the message. "Why don't you go over there and check on her." At least one of us should.

"What about you?" She asks standing up and gathering her things.

"What about me?"

She rolls her eyes, shaking her head. "Are you going to get your girl back? Eww, nope. Nope. I need another word. It's still weird to think about."

I offer a small smile. "Does this mean you give us your blessing?" I ask hopefully. Maybe things are getting better, and time would be on our side this time.

"I'm not saying I want to see you guys' lip locks or whatever. You can keep it to yourselves. But I'm not going to stand in the way of you guys' happiness either. I love you. And I love her. So, if it makes you happy I can get on board. It'll just take some time to get used to." Time, I could give her. And that's more than I could ever hope for. I feel a piece of my heart lift knowing I haven't lost anyone.

"Thank you," I choke over a ball of emotion that's wedged in my throat. "That means more to me than you'll ever know."

"Yeah, yeah. Now let's figure out a plan to get Serena back. Hopefully, this will earn me some brownie points with her too." I can hear how guilty she feels for the way she's treated Willow. I, too, hope they can work things out. Not for me. But for each other.

"Alright, let's go," I say as I grab my keys and we head out the door. My feet feel lighter than ever before. Not everything is resolved but I feel like I'm one step closer. "Thank you."

"Yeah, I can only help with Willow. Mom and Greyson are another story." She gives me a knowing look. She knows they'll be harder to win over.

I'm hopeful I'll have just as much luck as I did with Serena.

One thing at a time.

13

JAMES

1 Year Ago

"Trust me, Willow, you'll look hot," Serena walked past me as she held the phone to her. She breezed through the kitchen, stopping at the refrigerator to pull out a Diet Coke. I came by Elaine's house, which used to be mine, but in the divorce, I gave her the house. I came over talk about the last papers we needed to sign to make the divorce final. It's still a little awkward being here after I moved out. It didn't make sense to fight over who got the house. I didn't need the space the house afforded us and opted to rent an apartment in the city that overlooked Maine's skyline.

I was perched on the chair by the island in the middle of the massive kitchen for the past twenty minutes while I waited for Elaine to come down to talk over some last-minute stuff when I heard Serena mention Willow's name. My ears pricked in attention, dying to hear why Willow needed to look hot. I felt every inch of my body spark at the possibility of new information.

I had spoken to Willow last night over chips and dip as we watched some movie about a sinking boat and a couple who honestly should've survived the frigid temperatures of the sea had she switched places with him instead of hogging the board, or whatever she was laying on. According to Willow, it was an old movie, but the theaters loved playing "classics" late at night.

She had just finished an all-nighter for her job, and I had been up going over my business account trying to keep it afloat. Owning a new business was a lot harder than I originally planned for it to be, spending early mornings getting up before my employees to go over the days agenda and seeing if I can move things around for customers who hadn't made an appointment and even longer nights staying up to see if we made it into the black and checking over everything twice. There's an added layer of pressure when everything rides on you to make things successful. I only hired two mechanics to see how things would pan out. I didn't want to have too much money coming out before there was money going in. More times than not, I found myself with Willow staying up even later and talking about our day. For a woman as young as she was, she had a good head on her shoulders and had such a clear vision of the life she wants.

Our talks turned into late night food runs as we talked about anything and everything on our minds. Hearing she's getting dolled up stirs some curious feelings in my chest, leaving my skin feel tight and uncomfortable. My ears strain trying to hear any other clues on Willow's whereabouts.

"No, you have to wear the red dress. It makes your hair stand out and your butt look damn good in it. He will be drooling all over you." Serena's voice drifts further apart as she moves back upstairs to her old bedroom.

Although We Shouldn't

He?

She's going out with a guy? I wonder why she hadn't mentioned it to me. I mean we were casual friends, right? At least, I had considered her a friend. I've told her things I wouldn't dare voice to anyone else. And I thought she shared the same with me. So why didn't she tell me?

I didn't even know she was open to seeing anyone else since her breakup. I thought we were both on the mend after a disastrous relationship ending. Apparently not, since she was going to wear things that made her ass look good. Even though I thought it always looked good. I paused at the thought floating in my head.

Where the hell did that come from?

When did I begin to notice the way she looked? She was always a beautiful person but noticing how great her ass looks and okay, sure I made a few mental notes on the small patch of skin that showed when she reached for things too high. And—oh my god, I may have a thing for my daughters best friend.

My body swayed to the direction Serena walked to and had wondered who this new guy was. A buzzing irritation floated through my system, and I had the urge to storm over there to Willow and demand she call off the date. But that was nonsense. I couldn't do that. Could I?

"What crawled up your ass?"

I turned toward Elaine and plastered on a fake smile. "Nothing."

Her eyes scanned my face, determining whether she wanted to press the issue. She shakes her head and mutters something about bananas and men. "Anyway, what else do we need to do for things to be final. I still can't believe we're getting divorced." Her fruity smell of peaches and cream drifts over to me and I realize it does nothing for me. No butterflies. No warm tingly feeling.

It's strange how things are all coming full circle at the most inopportune moment.

I am no longer in love with my soon-to-be ex-wife, and I have feelings for my daughter's best friend.

Clearing my throat, I turn back to the papers I had brought with me. "We just need our signatures here and to file them with the court and we'll be free." It felt weird to say that out loud. Like we were imprisoned together. We had some good times, so it felt unfair to label it that way. We will no longer have any legal ties to one another. Only tied by our kids.

"If that's what you want," she offers a small smile and pushes a piece of her hair behind her ear. I used to find the gesture endearing. Now I feel nothing at all.

I nod my head toward the paper and offer a pen for her to sign. After the first mediation appointment we had, we came to a truce of sorts. As long as we compromised on some things, there was no need for anymore arguments.

She takes the pen from me and glances over the documents before signing her initials. "All done." Placing the pen back down, she sighs heavily. "We're finally divorced."

I feel relief as the weight of our relationship floats away. Seeing her fidget with her fingers, I walk up to her and give her a hug. "It'll be fine. Now you can focus on the things that matter to you without worrying about if I'm in the way. What matters is we can still see our kids."

"You're right," she smiles, but it looks forced.

"You don't have to sleep with him. But if you're feeling frisky, embrace your sexuality, chica. Who cares what people think?" Serena breezes back down with a pair of silver heels in her hand. "Thank you for letting us borrow these shoes, Mom. It will go great with Willow's outfit tonight." Serena hugs her mom before leaving out the door.

Fuck. Is it hot in here? Willow can't seriously be consid-

Although We Shouldn't

ering sleeping with this guy. He probably doesn't even know where to put his limp Dick. My heart speeds up at the images floating through my head.

"Hey, are you okay?" Elaine places her hand on my arm, and it feels like molten lava.

I move my arm. It feels wrong. All wrong. Willow shouldn't be out a date with anyone but me. For a while, I didn't know I was ready to date. I thought my heart was forever closed off after Elaine and I called it quits. But thinking of getting with Willow seems right. Like I should've seen the signs all along.

"James?" she calls out.

"Listen, it was great. But I have to go." My body moves off the stool, walking to the door. I should apologize for my brisk departure, but I can't right this second. I have to get out of here.

I waited a good forty minutes before finding myself standing outside of Cafe De Fleur. the owners named the restaurant due to the overabundance of flowers they have inside for decorations. The prices are pretty standard, not too high, and the food is pretty good too. Walking up to the hostess, I wait for her to seat me and then take my seat. She drops a menu down on the table and leaves me be.

I shouldn't be here. Willow might find it creepy and wonder how I knew where she was. It might have something to do with driving around town until I saw her through the window of the restaurant. I was operating off instinct and letting my mind take over. I had no plan or idea what I was going to do next. The only thing I knew was I needed to be here.

I'll only stay for a little while, I promised. Only long

enough to make sure she's safe and the guy doesn't try anything with her. It was a good plan. A solid plan. I lasted up until we finished our dinner course. The restaurant was small enough that I could see her two tables over, her back facing me. It also meant I could see his hand from where he was sitting inching towards her leg.

"Don't fucking think about it," I muttered stabbing my steak. My hand gripped the fork as I roughly bit off a piece of my food.

Willow scooted back out of his reach, and I loosened my breath. I felt like a mad man waiting to snap. Deep down, I knew my actions were irrational. But I was completely hopeless to stop them. I saw Willow excuse herself for the bathroom and got up and followed her.

I waited outside the bathroom for her to come out and leaned against the wall. With my eyes off of the jerk, I had time to process my actions. What was I doing following her here? If she wanted me to know she was on this date she would have told me. If some jerk did this to my daughter, I'd tell her to tell him to fuck off. Probably have a restraining order on him to teach him a lesson.

I knew these things yet couldn't find it in myself to walk away. What was it about her that had me doing things I wouldn't normally do? I didn't have time to ponder the question since she walked out the bathroom and bumped into me.

"James, what are you doing here?" her soft silky voice washed over me and calmed all the erratic thoughts in my head. She looked fucking beautiful in a red skintight dress that dipped in a v for some cleavage, and the silver heels Serena had fit perfectly on Willow's feet. Her hair was up in some elegant half up half down hairdo girls loved to wear, and her eyes had soft brown makeup on.

She smelled of citrus and spice, which made the pulse

Although We Shouldn't

beat rapidly in my neck. At the thought of this punk getting to see her in a way I hadn't before I growled.

Her eyes widened in surprise.

"Why didn't you tell me you were on a date?" My voice was rough and deep as I barely held myself back from tangling my hands in her wispy blonde hair. She swallowed and my eyes tracked the movement down her throat.

"I didn't know about it until Serena got home. She set me up on a blind date." Her eyes held mine, clasping her fingers together nervously.

Sure, we had hung out a few times and shared laughs but never had either of us dared to bring up the unhidden tension that floated through us. The stolen glances she gave me when I wasn't looking. All the times I gave her a few cursory glances and stored it in my memory. I had chalked it up to curiosity of our newfound friendship. I knew better now.

"Remind me to have a talk with my daughter about the dangers of meeting random men." I fisted my hands in my pocket when staying still wasn't working for me.

I felt the tension between us wind around the room, radiating off a nervous energy. At any minute it might snap and who knows what might happen next.

"I think he works at her bank or something," She steps closer to me. An unspoken question in her eye. What is this between us? Why are you really here? "It's not working out anyway. I'm not feeling it."

My eyes closed before the words tumbled out of my mouth. "Leave with me." The moment they left my lips it felt right. I let the words settle between us before finding her eyes again.

"I can't just leave." She stammers, her hands sweeping in her hair.

I felt my control snap as I backed her up against the wall

behind her. We were nothing more than an inch apart. Our breaths mingled with another as we both danced on the imaginary line between us. "Leave with me." I said again. Daring her to cross the line with me.

"What about him?" she asked, fishing for a way out of the situation we found ourselves in.

"Leave with me." My voice was smoother and surer as I held her eyes and finally—finally—tangled my hand in her hair and titled her face up with me. She licked her lips, smearing a little of her red lipstick off and I tracked the movement like she was my prey. In a way she was. Now that I have my sights set on her, I was zeroed in on her every movement.

Anticipation thrummed in my veins as I inched even closer to her. I never felt more alive than I had in this second. It felt like everything depended on her next choice. *Will she or won't she?* She held her breath and I leaned down and inhaled her scent. My nose drifted along the column of her neck. She shivered under my touch, letting me know she wasn't immune to my touch. How long have I wondered what this was between us? How long if I wondered if we were just friends? I splayed my hands on her belly as I choked on my words. "Leave with me."

She searched my eyes, for I don't know what. But whatever she saw must've been all she needed to see before she nodded her head and whispered, "Okay."

My self-control snapped and like a magnet, my lips pulled down on hers, capturing her lips in a soft caress. Electricity sparkled between us, like friction built up and ready to implode.

Her hands were soft and hesitant as they figured out where to land on me before finally deciding to land on my shoulders. I felt everything in me sigh and scream mine. It was an out of this world experience, like the angels signing from above. My body demanded for more AS I drank in each of her soft sighs.

Pulling away, I waited for her eyes to open as she gave me a soft, shy smile.

This was crazy.

I might go to hell for these feelings, and damn that kiss would last me a lifetime. But I knew within those sixty seconds of heaven, I would gladly send my soul to hell for more moments like this.

Because I could never go back, now that I know how fucking right she feels next to me.

14

WILLOW

A picture is worth a thousand words. I wonder what it says that the only place that brings me any sort of comfort is Tony's pizzeria. The smell of freshly made pizza sauce fills the air making my already sensitive stomach bubble. I used to love the smell of Tony's ooey gooey madness, which he perfected over time for his infamous pizzas. I could scarf down two full boxes. By the way my stomach is reacting to the scents, I could barely get down a slice. Still, I can't find it in me to walk away and go home.

It's been awfully quiet since Serena hasn't been back. She used to play music way too loud as she was getting ready. I have no one to talk to. Aside from my brother, who I corralled into coming here with. Cameron is a big softie. One look at my blotchy red eyes and he couldn't say no to me. At least he can eat with no problem. I couldn't really blame him, though.

Tony's pizzas were delicious.

Two pink lines haunt me as I stare down at my wrapped pregnancy test.

"Do you need another ginger ale?" Cameron asked, taking a huge chunk out of his next pizza slice.

I'm jealous. I would love to stuff my face in my favorite extra cheesy pizza like I used to for every break-up. But the only thing I can even vaguely keep down is water or ginger ale in this joint. Luckily, I brought a pack of crackers to nibble on.

My eyes squint as I consider how much ginger ale is in my cup. "No thanks, I still have half a cup left. I'll wait and see how I feel after." I pull out another saltine and nibble on it.

He sighs. "So, when are you going to tell him?" He asks, referring to my baby news.

I divulged the whole truth about James and I when I went to his place in need of comfort. I spent the first two weeks at his apartment hiding out. At first, he was shocked at the at how long I had kept our affair a secret. I expected him to be disappointed or at the least wary of our relationship. He's always been protective of me. Instead, he looked at me and said, "Not once have you come to me crying about how bad things were. That alone tells me he's a good guy. Despite the age gap."

I think I needed to hear that more than I knew. It felt like a Mack truck was lifted off me. It was the first time since everything went down that I allowed myself to admit we were great together.

I shrug, hesitant to even come up with a game plan to even think about telling anyone else about my pregnancy. "I need some time. Everything has been so heavy lately. And my first appointment is in a couple of days. Let me get through that, then I can think about everything else I have to do." I rub my temples as I concentrate on breathing through my nose. My nausea has been a bitch lately. It feels like the content of my stomach has been doing somersault rolls.

Although We Shouldn't

Leaning back, I close my eyes and try to get through the next wave.

My brother pushes something towards me, and I look down to see another cup of ginger ale. My eyes teared up. Before I can thank him, I bolt out of my seat and run to the bathroom. There's no way I can make it another second. Despite my best efforts, the nausea won out.

Once I get to a bathroom stall, I drop to my knees and expel everything out. Great. This about sums up my life so far. I feel my phone in my pocket vibrate. Pulling it out, I see another call from James. I hit "ignore call" before sliding it back in my pocket. Another day, James. I wish I had the luxury of being in his arms and crying to him about the recent development of our relationship. Until he figures out what he's going to do with his family, I can't go to him.

I need to figure this out on my own.

Once my stomach has settled enough and I know nothing else will come out, I stand and exit the stall. Splashing some water on my face, I take a good look in the mirror. I don't recognize the girl staring back at me. Her eyes are hollow and distant. Her skin is pale and blotchy from crying. My once shiny hair is not dull and limp from not washing it. It's tossed in a hap hazard bun. Oh well. It's not like I have anyone to impress. Popping a mint in my mouth, I head back to my table.

I'll tell Cameron that we can take the rest of the food to go. As much as I love sitting in here, I can't take it another second. It's not worth the nausea I've experienced here. Only when I GET TO our table, he's not there. Serena and James are. My heart speeds up in my chest. What are they doing here? Did my brother leave me? He must've, that can only be the next possible explanation.

Not wanting to interrupt their time together, I head for the door. At least they're patching things up. I'm happy for them. I feel more tears bubbling in my eyes. As I get closer to the exit, I hear my name being called. *It's your mind playing tricks on you. Don't believe it.*

"Willow," The voice gets louder. It sounds a lot like Serena. "Willow, over here."

Turning around, I see her wave me over. I gulp. I'm nervous as to why she's suddenly speaking to me again. She sits back down in her seat but offers a reassuring smile, waiting for me to come over. And James? God James's eyes still hold me captive. He's dark and moody. I wonder if this was his idea or Serena's. Hesitant footsteps lead me toward them, as I stand in front of them awkwardly. I don't know what I'm doing here.

Serena points to the opposite side of the table from where she and James sit and I plop down. If this is my walking plank, at least I get to say goodbye to the two most important people in my life.

Serena peeks between me and her father before pulling in a deep breath. "Let me just start off saying, I'm still confused about how this all came about. But I had a talk with my dad, and he explained that you guys never intended to hurt me."

My heartbeat thuds in my ears. I'm sure they can hear it going off in my chest. I placed my hands underneath my thighs, quelling the urge to take her hands. "I'm so sorry if we hurt you. I never wanted that to happen."

She nods. "I can accept that. What I can't accept is you hiding things from me. We're best friends. We tell each other everything." she cringes and looks at her dad. "Well not everything anymore. I would rather not hear the sordid details about you and my dad, thank you very much. But everything else—the big things. We tell each other. No matter how much it may hurt the other."

Her words bring hope as I glance at the two of them trying to make sense of what she's implying. "What are you saying?" I need her to tell it to me straight. I don't want to assume anything and make a fool of myself.

"What I'm saying is, I'm sorry." her eyes tear up. "I didn't mean it when I said we weren't friends. I should've started with that in the first place. But I'm also saying, it's going to take some time to get used to. But I'm okay with your relationship with my dad."

My eyes drift to James and only then does he break out into a smile. Oh my god. Is this really happening? As if he can read my thoughts he nods and gets up. I stand with him and slowly we make our way to each other like two magnets being pulled together. I feel his arms wrap around me and I cry tears of relief.

I thought for sure, things were over between us. That his family couldn't accept us. He placed a small kiss on my forehead and it my body melts off all the tension I've been keeping. When we sit back down, he sits next to me, instead of across.

Serena smiles. "That's really all I came for. To tell you, you have my blessing. As for the rest of my family, let the cards fall where they may. I'm pretty sure they're still upset. But I don't want to stand in the way of you guys' happiness." She stands to leave but stops before turning back to me. "Oh, your brother said to call him if you need him to pick you up. We kind of had to beg him to ambush you this way."

I laugh. It feels like my life has been a whirlwind of events. James grabbed my hands and placed them on the table and played with my fingers. "I thought I'd never get to hold your hands again." His deep voice wraps over me like a warm blanket, soothing all my frayed edges. He focuses on my bare ring finger and his brows pull.

"It's on chain around my neck," I pull the chain from underneath my shirt and show it to him. I couldn't fully let the idea of us go. But with so much uncertainty, it felt wrong to wear it on my finger, and even more wrong to not have it on me. I explain as much to him.

"I get that." He toys with the chain before yanking it off me and snapping the chain. I gasp, reaching for my neck. My protest dies on my lips as he places the ring squarely on my finger.

He holds up a finger cutting off anything I was going to say. "Let me say this first, because it needs to be said." I wait patiently as he gathers his thoughts, taking the time to drink my fill of him. All these weeks apart and it feels like I'm seeing him for the first time. When he finally spoke, his voice is smooth and steady as he stares deep into my eyes. "I knew getting into a relationship with you was the biggest risk of my life. I knew there were many things I had to deal with along the way. And though we have faced the biggest hurdle we would ever have to face, we didn't face them alone. We shouldn't face them alone. If you do this with me, and take me back, I promise to always hold your hand through the storm and bare as much of the weight as I can with you. Because not loving you is as impossible as the sun freezing over. You are ingrained in everything I am. You are the air I breathe, the wind gliding against my skin. You are forever tattooed on me, and your love will live in my soul for eternity. I refuse to give up someone so essential to my life. I love you. I will never stop loving you. Marry me, Willaford, and make me the luckiest son of a bitch in the world."

By the time he finishes his speech, tears stream down my face as I let out a watery laugh. This man has no idea the hold he has on me. I never really left. I have always been his. When words fail me, I nod my head, accepting his re-proposal, and reach out to him and kiss him. It feels like I have waited my entire life for this moment. Everything is just so…

Perfect.

Although We Shouldn't

Everything feels perfect.

His gentle hands wipe away the last of my tears as he gathers me in his arms. "We'll figure the rest out later. All that matters is we're finally together with no more secrets. Nothing else that can hold us back." His words sound like music to my ears, although I'm currently sitting on the biggest secret of them all. Our baby.

I wait a few minutes to collect my thoughts. I had no idea how he'd react to the news, he already had kids of his own that are well past college. What if he didn't want to go through that process all over again. Nerves gathered in my stomach as I thought of all the possible ways that I could tell him about our unexpected surprise.

"There's actually something I need to tell you." My mouth felt like I had a bag of cotton stuff in my mouth. I reached for the water bottle that was on the table and took a sip to quell the bubbling anxiety that took flight in my nervous system.

"You can tell me anything," his fingers still had a hold of me as he brushed his fingers along my wrist, taking me off the ledge.

Just tell him. What's the worst that'll happen? He could leave, my mind so kindly offers up. Except, looking at him and the earnestness in his eyes, I know that isn't true. This man wouldn't have risked upsetting his family—the one permanent thing in life—to be with me. He wouldn't be sitting in front of me today, asking me to marry him all over again only to run at the news of a baby.

With that thought in mind I steeled my spine. "I'm pregnant." I placed his hands on my stomach, that wasn't showing yet, but I already had all the love in the world for my precious bundle of joy. "I'm having our baby." The air around us was silent while I waited for him to speak—to say anything.

And when he did, he didn't disappoint. "If it's anything

like its mother, I will love it twice as much as I do her." His eyes tear up. "You have no idea how happy I am to hear this."

"You're not mad?"

"The only thing I'm mad about is not being there when you found out the news." He coughs to hide his sobs. "This kid is going to be loved so much."

Sitting here in the one place that nursed all my heartbreaks throughout my teenaged angst-filled life, I felt restored and renewed. I had the love of my life waiting for me to start our life together and a baby in my belly, making us a family.

A kiss was always more than a kiss.

It told a story to the recipient. It brought all kinds of ends and beginnings. As James brought his lips to mine and unified our future, I knew without a doubt this kiss meant forever.

And always.

THE END

Want to read more romance?
Read the small-town romance for Micheal and Morgan in The Sweet Spot.

SAMPLE CHAPTER ONE FROM THE SWEET SPOT

Morgan

This can't be right.

Sitting in my company van, my eyes are fixed on a black sports car parked in the driveway of the house I'm supposed to be delivering these delicious red velvet with chocolate swirl frosting cupcakes to. The problem is this car seems identical to Scott's, my boyfriend of two years.

But it can't be. Just this morning he told me he'd be busy in back-to-back meetings with clients today.

He's a financial advisor at one of the most well-known companies in the top 500. I remember when he finally made it. He celebrated by buying the same exact car. He's also my financial advisor. As crazy as it seems, that's not how we met. We met at the grocery store while I was buying ingredients for my cupcakes when I was just starting up my company. I was in sweats, my then long brown hair was in a lopsided, messy bun, and I was in the dairy aisle looking for the best deal on almond milk for a new recipe I was trying out.

He had startled me from behind when I heard him say, "Nice bun."

Now naturally, I wasn't standing for some random man ogling my ass. So, in return, I glared my blue eyes at him sharply and responded, "Personal space, buddy." I wanted to say a lot more than what came out of my mouth, but the peacemaker in me wanted to deescalate the situation. Causing a scene in the grocery store wasn't my thing. And years of experience with being the pacifier in the family taught me being subtle was the best route.

He gave me a closed mouth smile, which was a little too smug for me, and said, "I was talking about your hair."

I looked at him skeptically, my mouth twisted in suspicion, not fully believing him until he explained that it was a great opening line for conversation. The more we talked, the more I warmed up to him. We were together for a full six months before he started helping me plan financially for my bakery.

Back in high school, I used to eat my way through my feelings with cakes and cookies. I'd lose myself and drown my emotions in the decadent tastes of my favorite treats such as the rich sweetness of the chocolate chips from the cookies or the uniquely balanced taste of the tart from the lemon mixed in with the soft gooey texture of the cream in the lemon meringue pie. Sweets became my safe haven. They got me through my awkward preteen years, the grueling high school years trying to find myself, and bonded me with my mom when she taught me the beauty of baking.

When it came time to apply for college, it was a no brainer I'd attend culinary school. It was where I took my abilities to the next level and really came into myself.

But back to my current predicament, I just can't shake the funny feeling in my belly I'm getting. It isn't the good kind, either. I furrow my brow, twisting my lips to the side in contemplation. Yes, I'm certain Scott told me he was busy up until 3 pm today. Checking the time on my phone, it reads

Although We Shouldn't

it's only 12:45 pm. It couldn't possibly be Scott's car. Besides, I've never known him to take personal appointments anyway. "Get a grip, girl," I mutter to myself quietly. Shaking my head of any lingering wayward thoughts, I grab the delivery order and take one last look at the delivery card that read:

Something sweet for someone naughty ;) to confirm the address.

It always makes me chuckle, and without fail, I did again just now, lightening the mounting tension I have in my belly. Climbing out of the van, I head towards the house. This was the second week I was trying out the delivery option to see how customers respond to it, and I want to deliver these on time. Approaching the porch steps to the house, I couldn't help but cast one last backward glance at that damn sports car.

Reaching the door, I exhale slowly and knock on the door as a zing of anticipation tingles in my body. Normally, I didn't do the deliveries, but my best friend and manager, Savannah, is at the store manning the front because one of my other girls was out sick. Today, I get to experience first-hand the smile on the customers' faces when they receive one of my delectable treats. It's a priceless feeling and can't be replaced with anything else.

Waiting for another five minutes as I shake my white blouse with my free hand, and attempt to control my sweat. It was unusually warm here in the early springtime in Bridgeview. Usually, we don't get our warmer weather until May. And it was only March right now. Thank goodness this was the only delivery today; otherwise, I would have to rethink my entire outfit. My company van is refrigerated so any other deliveries would be safe. Thank God for small favors.

I place another closed-fist knock on the door, giving the

owner of the house another chance to answer the door. As I was about to leave, I hear something permeating through the door. It sounds like someone fell. A slight thud coming from the front of the house. Concerned, I swivel my head left and right to see if anyone was around to help. But I'm the only one outside at the moment. Hesitantly, I reach for the doorknob, unsure if it was the right thing to do, remembering the sense of foreboding that was in my belly. Giving the doorknob a twist, I find it unlocked and open it.

And there I see the culprit of the sound I heard through the door. Someone hadn't fallen. A couple was lost in the last throes of pleasure. Not just any couple, either, but the man was Scott.

My Scott.

Supposed to be in a meeting, Scott.

Confirming what I already know, there on his wrist is the limited-edition silver watch I had gotten him for his birthday just last month. The same one he had said wasn't the best gift he had gotten, although I had saved every hard-earned penny, I had to buy it for him. He's currently balls deep in a leggy—and—quite busty—redhead with her top half exposed and her skirt bunched up to her waist. Now, Scott is another story. He was completely naked, minus his damn watch.

They're just in the entryway on the bottom steps, like they couldn't wait to be with each other and started there. I hear Scott bottoming out on her, nearing the end, and sounding mighty pleased with himself.

"Dear God, Mandy, damn, this is so good," he groans out, eye clenched shut, head thrown back as he pumps the last few times behind her. It can just be heard over her high-pitched moans.

Mandy.

So, that's the name of my demise. And the complete opposite of me.

Although We Shouldn't

She's beautiful.

I had been so sure that Scott only had eyes for me. But clearly, that doesn't mean that he *only* desires me. Nor had it meant that I was enough for him. I'll never forget the way she sounds while he brings her to her own orgasm.

I'm currently comparing her sex sounds to mine, wondering whose he prefers more. They must've felt the draft from the main door still being open. Or the cupcake I just thrown in their direction that landed in his hair, because they turn around and Scott gapes at me, eyes bulging comically wide.

"Morgan?! What are you doing here?" he bellows. Yes, that's the correct question to ask. Like I am the one at fault here.

Mandy takes this as the opportunity to tell him just why I'm here. "Oh good, my cupcake deliveries," she announces, her eyes lighting in delight. She was either stupid or intentionally oblivious to the tension thickening in the room.

"Me? What are you doing here? With *her*," I scream, casting a withering glare in Mandy's direction. She's lucky stares can't lay harm, otherwise she'd be dead.

Scott holds up his hands in a placating gesture, as if it would magically calm the situation. "I can explain. Mandy wanted a personal consultation, and this wasn't supposed to happen. I swear. It was just this one time," he tries to appease me. "I don't know how we got to this point."

I scoff and roll my eyes. I throw another cupcake in his direction, and it lands on Ms. Perfect Boob's D cup breast. Score. That feels so satisfying. "It." *Hit.* "Doesn't." *Hit.* "Matter," *HIT, HIT.* I'm not really paying attention to where they land, it just feels good to get this out of my system.

Mandy slithers up from behind Scott, looking like she was trying to reach for *my* cupcakes, and I shoot another glare at her, which stops her from coming any closer. Good.

I feel something wet trickle down my face, and I swipe it off.

Tears.

Just great. There are tears traveling down my face. How humiliating.

I'm still staring at Scott in utter dismay when I decide it isn't worth it. I throw the remainder of the cupcakes toward them and run out the door to my van. Scott starts to give chase but stops at the entranceway when he notices he is still without any form of clothing on, and just starts yelling my name as I drive away.

With a million thoughts running through my mind, I drive around restlessly for a while, my tears still cascading down my face, blurring my vision. Now that I'm alone, it doesn't matter my eyes are competing to be the world's largest waterfall. He doesn't deserve my emotions anymore. Not when he shared his with another. I stop near a park, getting out, and walk along the trail. I suck in a staggering breath as I silently cry my eyes out. "How could he," I ask no one in particular. I was alone. No one would answer me. Or could, for that matter.

Great, where am I going to live now? Our apartment is out of the question. And it's way too last minute to find one by myself.

I pull out my phone and send Ben, my older brother, a text message.

ME: 911.

He's the fixer of our family. Ben, the lawyer, always knows what to do. He helped me form the idea to open my bakery. He helped our younger brother, Theodore, start his DJ career with his best friend, Charlie. And for the youngest, Faith, Ben helped her with anything she needed help with. If she ever asked for help. My phone pings with a new text alert.

Although We Shouldn't

Ben: What's the emergency?

I dry my eyes of its newest tears to reply. **I need a new place to stay. Scott and I are over.**

I was expecting another text reply from him when I park my bottom on a bench, but instead, he calls.

Sucking in a fortifying breath to calm myself, I answer the phone. I don't want to alert him that I'm crying. He brings a whole new meaning to overprotective.

"What do you MEAN you need another place to stay?" he answers with a raised voice. Which is never a good sign. He's normally calm and collected.

"I caught Scott with another woman. IN another woman," I mutter miserably, I sniffle hard as my vision clouds over again. No matter how much I try to hold it in, a few hiccups escape. This isn't happening. He's the one guy whom I believed really thought I was truly beautiful. That makes me *feel* beautiful.

At least, he used to.

Ben utters a curse under his breath as he roughly exhales. "Hey, I'm going to get you through this. Just pack what you can into your car, and we'll arrange for somewhere for you to stay." He softens his voice, probably noticing I was still crying, "It's going to be okay, Morg, he doesn't deserve you."

"Yeah," I say again, letting out another sob, unconvinced. We end the call, and I muffle my cries with my head in my hands. This sucks. He's the only boyfriend I've ever had, and I couldn't even manage to hold his attention.

Today is beautiful. The sun is out, the skies are blue with fluffy white clouds, a slight breeze swirling around. And on a day where I should be enjoying the weather and the first delivery I could deliver myself, I was heartbroken. My mascara is running down my face from excessively crying, and my eyeliner is probably smudged. I glance down at my shirt haphazardly and notice, to top it all off, I managed to smear chocolate frosting on my shirt.

Great, my insides match my outsides.

Messing with the stain, I try to wipe it off without making it worse. In the midst of my pity party, I feel something nudge my ankle. Glancing down, I spot a chocolate giving me the biggest smile with his tongue hanging out the side of his mouth. He has the most beautiful brown coat of fur I've ever seen on a chocolate lab. He nudges my hand, begging me to give him some rubs. Strangely, it's just what I need to pick up my day.

"Hey, handsome, where did you come from?" I coo to him, as I rub his head. His tongue hangs out the side of his mouth as he leans into my hand. He whines and puts a paw on my lap, as if lending a supporting hand for me. He doesn't have a name tag on him, but I'm sure this gorgeous guy belongs to someone.

He hops up, standing on his two hind legs, and licks my face, letting out a bark. He's almost all the way in my lap, but I don't care. I'll take anything he does, willing his happiness to wear off on me.

Then, I hear it. The most beautiful, deep, soothing sound I've ever heard. As the voice gets closer to me, my heart speeds up in my chest, and I see the dog's ear perk up. A few minutes later, the most gorgeous man I've ever seen approaches me. Well, not me. But the dog.

"There you are, Rufus. I stopped jogging for one minute, and you couldn't wait for me." Though he sounds like he's scolding the dog, it also holds a hint of amusement in his tone. He's shirtless and wearing black basketball shorts and white Nike shoes. Abs staring back at me, and a happy trail peeking out from the top of his shorts. *Goddamn.* He bends down on one knee, ruffling the top of Rufus's head, and clips his leash on. With Rufus secure, he eyes hold me hostage and

Although We Shouldn't

I'm blinded by the intensity of his stare. He has the most gorgeous hazel eyes with a hint of brown in his irises and light brown hair, a soft caramel color. "Hey," he directs at me, leaving me momentarily stunned, his voice smooth and alluring.

I suddenly forget twenty minutes ago I had just discovered I was left single and completely homeless for the time being. All I can focus on is the gorgeous man in front of me.

"Hi," I whisper, still staring at him, hooked.

His eyes crinkle at the corners, eyes sparkling in the sunlight, looking like an Adonis, and smiles at me warmly. "Sorry about that," he apologizes. "Rufus here can't resist a lady in distress. He feeds off emotions." He glances down at his dog, and the dog bows his head in confirmation. I have to admit, the pair is cute.

Be still, my beating heart.

I lift a shoulder and simultaneously wipe my face on my blouse. Then, it dawns on me the current state I'm in, train wreck and all. I feel my cheeks heat in embarrassment, and I wince. Just great, as if my luck can get any worse.

As if he can sense my inner turmoil, he wipes a streak of mascara off my cheek and tucks an errant hair behind my ear. "Still beautiful," he said softly, and the dog whines some more, leaning his head against my knee in agreement. "The most gorgeous brown eyes to have ever gotten lost in."

I roll those so-called brown eyes in annoyance. "They're actually blue. I'm wearing contacts." Scott thinks I look better with brown eyes to match my mousy brown hair. He's also the reason I had cut my hair a few inches shorter at shoulder length. Another reason to hate the rat bastard. He lifts my chin and gazes directly into my eyes, not letting me escape his penetrating gaze.

"And I bet they're beautiful, too," he says somberly.

"I don't know about that." I break our gaze, the intensity too much for me at the moment.

"Well, I do."

The background noise that originally faded away comes rushing back, along with the sound of my phone going off with frequent text alerts. I sigh inwardly. Looks like Ben started up the family group chat and alerted the gang. *Crap.*

He glances between my eyes with his brows lowered. "What's wrong?" A frown forms on his face, whether it's in confusion or concern, I'm not sure.

I must've spoken the thought out loud. Instead of answering him, I rifle through my purse and locate my phone. Stray papers and gum wrappers spill out, tumbling around me. Ten new text messages. Yep, definitely the group text.

Ben: Who has a spare room that Morgan can bunk in?

Theo: I'm sharing with Charlie. And the rest of the apartment houses our DJ equipment.

Theo: Didn't she just move in with her boyfriend?

Ben: Yeah, it's no longer an option. They broke up.

Theo: Awe, I'm sorry, Morg. Maybe Faith has a spare.

Fay: I have room. It's usually just me in my apartment.

Ben: Good, it's all set. Morgan, we'll help you pack the rest of your stuff later on today.

Fay: Love you, sissy.

Fay: Slumber party tonight.

I can always count on Faith for a pick me up. But the last text is from Scott.

Scott: Come home.

Yeah, right. I sigh heavily, the weight of the worries pressing upon me and my thoughts battling each other in my head. "Everything okay?" I startle, forgetting he was still crouched in front of me.

I give a weak smile, brushing my hair out of my face.

Although We Shouldn't

"Yeah, it will be," I say dejectedly. I laugh mockingly, "Sorry about all this." I motion toward my outward appearance and shrug as if it's all the explanation I need.

"It's okay." He smiles again, and this time flashes his pearly whites. Double damn, he's a double threat, triple if you count the dog. "My name is Michael" He stands and reaches his hand out for me to shake. I place my hand in his, and a jolt of electricity runs through me.

Standing back up, I tell him my name, "Morgan." I check the time on my phone and sigh once more. Reluctantly, I pull my hands away, though his hands are having a hard time letting go as well. I clear my throat. "Sorry, I have to go," I mumble before rushing away.

"I hope to see you again, Morgan," he calls after me.

Yes, me too.

And like the heavens were tempting me, I cast a backward glance back at him. He's still there, staring at me with his dog walking circles around him.

Yea. this is the worst luck I could have today. First, my boyfriend cheats on me. And now I have to walk away from a beautiful man.

If my luck couldn't get any worse.

To read more, pick up The Sweet Spot on Amazon today!

BOOKS BY GWEN PARKS

Sometimes Love Series
The Sweet Spot
Trusted Tempo

Standalone
Hidden Affairs

KEEP IN TOUCH WITH GWEN PARKS

Reader Group
Website
Bookbub
Amazon
Instagram
Tiktok
Facebook
Goodreads
Sign up for Gwen's mailing list to receive exclusive updates, content, and giveaways!
Newsletter

ABOUT THE AUTHOR

Gwen Parks is a book enthusiast who loves reading and writing happily ever afters. She writes New Adult and contemporary romance stories that pulls the reader in and leaves you rooting for them. She put a realistic spin on her stories that are relatable to the reader. She loves a good book that will leave her crying her heart out and wishing there was a part two to continue the story.

On a good (preferably sunny) day, you can find her at the dog park watching her three dogs enjoy life and eating ice cream while it's cold. She prides herself on connecting with other readers and loves to chat about a good book.

When she's not distracted by her fur babies and not working on her next book, she's busy daydreaming about her next travel adventure. Currently, she has her sights set on Europe. So be on the lookout!

Made in the USA
Columbia, SC
29 September 2024